SHADOWS OF
CONFLICT

By the same author

Follow Your Star
Rendezvous in Cannes

Shadows of Conflict

Jennifer Bohnet

ROBERT HALE · LONDON

© Jennifer Bohnet 2013
First published in Great Britain 2013

ISBN 978-0-7198-0876-0

Robert Hale Limited
Clerkenwell House
Clerkenwell Green
London EC1R 0HT

www.halebooks.com

2 4 6 8 10 9 7 5 3 1

Typeset in 11.25/17.5pt New Century Schoolbook
Printed by MPG Printgroup, UK

'... This was a people's war,
And everyone was in it.'

COLONEL OVETA CULP HOBBY

ONE

'Take over your shop?' Katie Teague said, looking at her godmother, Mattie. 'Are you serious?'

'Never more so. Shop needs dragging into the twenty-first century,' Mattie said. 'I don't have the energy any more.' Or the inclination, she could have added, but didn't.

'You're not ill?' Katie glanced at her sharply. Mattie didn't look ill but some people still looked in the best of health when they died, didn't they?

'Not ill – just tired. The shop needs a young person's input. You need a job, don't you? I promise not to interfere and I'll give you a completely free hand to do what you want.' Mattie replaced her tea cup on the saucer.

'In fact I shall take my first ever summer holiday this year if you take over. More cream with that scone?'

The two of them were sitting in Mattie's secluded garden overlooking the River Dart and enjoying the usual spread of food that Mattie considered essential for a proper Sunday afternoon tea: scones, Devonshire splits, clotted cream and her home-made strawberry jam. Bert, her Labradoodle, sat at their feet, ready to guzzle up any stray crumb that might come his way.

'Oh, Mattie,' Katie said. 'I don't know. I was planning on a couple of weeks' holiday before sending off more job applications. Can't say I'd even considered coming back here to live permanently.'

'Well, think about it now. Give yourself a year to get A Good Yarn back into shape and then we'll decide whether you take it on permanently – or whether we sell up and split the profits.'

'Isn't there anyone else willing to give you a hand?' Katie asked.

'There's only Leo and somehow I don't see him running the place.'

Katie smiled at the thought of Leo Cranford, Mattie's nephew and her teenage sparring partner, working in the wool shop. It would simply never happen.

Mattie stood up.

'I'll fetch another pot of tea while you decide.'

'No pressure then,' Katie said.

'Of course not. But the holiday season is only weeks away. Be good to have things organized by then.'

Waiting for the kettle to boil, Mattie stood by the kitchen window deep in thought, praying that Katie would take on the shop. Watching her now in the garden, Mattie crossed her fingers and willed Katie to make the decision she wanted her to make.

Left on her own, Katie wandered along the garden path, Bert at her heels. From the vantage point by the wall at the top of the garden, she had a good view of the activity on the river. The Lower Ferry making its way across the river, the tourist boats returning from Totnes, the marinas packed to capacity with boats. It was all achingly familiar – and yet so different from when she was growing up down here.

Then there had only been the one marina up by the shipyard and a couple of pontoons moored mid-river downstream by the Higher Ferry, from where her uncle Frank had run his boat charters. These days the harbour master had his hands full controlling the coming's and goings of leisure boats of all sizes from the several marinas now lining the banks of the river.

There was so much more going on in the town these days too. It was no longer the sleepy riverside town she'd been determined to escape from as a teenager and find life. In the last few years life itself had arrived down here while she'd been busy pursuing a career up in Bristol – a career that had been jettisoned by her recent redundancy.

She still felt numb when she remembered her last afternoon in the office. Hugo had called a midday meeting and without warning told three of them their contracts were being terminated with immediate effect. He'd handed them all envelopes with their final payments and a reference, together with the instruction to clear their desks.

Patrick, standing at Hugo's side, had avoided her gaze. It wasn't until Hugo had left and Katie was bemusedly packing her things into a box that he came into her office.

'You knew this was going to happen, didn't you? Why didn't you warn me? You're my boyfriend, for God's sake.' She threw an out-of-date copy of *Campaign* into the wastepaper basket. 'You're not going to tell me you didn't know? You practically run this place for Hugo.'

Patrick shook his head. 'I'm sorry, Katie. I honestly didn't know until this morning that you were included. Besides, how could I say anything to Hugo without him guessing that you and I are more than colleagues? He'd have sacked you then anyway. You know what the rules about office romances are.'

'He might have sacked you, not me!' Katie retorted, knowing full well that that would never have happened. Patrick was too big a part of the agency. His contacts book was full of names and telephone numbers of all the big hitters in the industry. Patrick knew the people who really mattered.

Keeping their affair a secret for the past six months had been romantic at first but lately Katie had begun to suspect that Patrick was perhaps using the 'no couples in the office' rule as an excuse for them not moving in together. Maybe Hugo did know about them and that's why he hadn't told Patrick his plan to include her in his redundancies?

As if sensing her thoughts, Patrick put his arms around her. 'There will be benefits about not working here. We can 'come out' now about you and me, when you're working in another office.'

'If I can find another job,' Katie said. 'You know what the work situation is like down here. The last thing I want to do is move to London.' Big cities were not her scene. Bristol was large enough for her any day.

'Something will turn up. I'll put some feelers out, see what I can find. Come on, cheer up, Katie, it's not the end of the world. You've got a good redundancy package there.'

'But I want a job. I like being a film production manager.'

'You'll get one soon enough. Trust me,' Patrick had said.

He had then helped her carry the box to her car. And so the last five years of her working life had ended.

That was two weeks ago and neither she nor Patrick had managed to uncover any likely jobs – which was why she'd decided to visit Mattie and have a short holiday. Since her parents had retired to Spain seven years ago her visits home had dwindled down to one or two a year, a fact which she felt increasingly guilty over as she knew Mattie missed her visits.

The idea of taking over A Good Yarn did have a certain appeal. She could regard it as a career break, something different to recharge the batteries. She could always go back to town if it didn't work out. Other people had career breaks, so why not her? Where would she live, though?

'Oh, what to do, Bert?' She stroked the dog as his black nose nudged her hand for attention. 'Shall I come back and take on Mattie's shop? Or shall I stay in Bristol and try going freelance until something permanent turns up?'

Mattie returned with the tea and a large key which she pushed across the table to Katie.

'Here,' she said. 'Take this and go have a look later.'

Katie picked up the key thoughtfully. 'What will you do if I don't take on the shop?'

'Run it right down over the summer and have a closing down sale at Christmas. Maybe see if the developers renovating the place next door are still interested.' Mattie shrugged. 'I've got another year to keep it out of the hands of the Blackawton cousins. Ron keeps harping on about getting his rights from the old war time family agreement.'

Katie looked at her. 'Ron? Family agreement?'

'Too long a story to go into now but I do know I'll be wracked with guilt if I do close mother's business after all these years even though it was always meant to be Clara's not mine. I never wanted it in the first place.'

'I thought you loved the shop, enjoyed working there. You're always knitting.' Strange, Katie thought, how mistaken you could be about people close to you.

'I didn't have a choice after the war and Clara was dead. Mother needed me. So here I stayed, knitting pins in hand,' Mattie said.

Katie remembered being scared of old Ma Cranford as a child. Secretly, she and Lara had nicknamed her the Witch and stayed as far away from her as possible. She could well understand a young Mattie all those years ago being made to toe the dutiful daughter line with no argument allowed.

'Don't go thinking it was all bad,' Mattie said. 'I enjoyed being in charge once Mother had died and I was running the business my way. But these days there are so many new rules and regulations. I guess, too, I'm not businesslike enough.'

Mattie glanced at Katie. 'Remember how you enjoyed being my Saturday girl for years. Lara too, before she got bitten by the sailing bug. Does she know you're redundant and down for a visit?'

'Had lunch with her last week,' Katie said. 'Dexter was away at a farming conference so we had a girly day. They'll be down in the summer so you'll see them then.'

Mattie laughed as she stood up and began to collect the tea things. 'I'll never forget those fluorescent stripy socks you both knitted one winter – orange and green. Your teachers were less than impressed when you wore them to school though!'

'I'd forgotten those,' Katie said. 'I did a lot of knitting and sewing in those days, didn't I?'

'Yes and that's why you're perfect to take on A Good Yarn. You know how to do things.'

'Oh, Mattie, just because I can turn the heel of a sock, doesn't mean I can run a wool shop,' Katie said, laughing. Or even if I want to, she refrained from adding.

Half an hour later Katie walked down through the narrow streets towards the river and Mattie's shop. A few people were wandering around enjoying the early evening sunshine. Negotiating the granite steps between Newcomen Road and Lower Street, Katie turned towards Bayards Cove.

Minutes later she was outside A Good Yarn, pushing the key into the lock. Once inside she instinctively reached for the light switch on the right-hand wall and pushed the door closed behind with her foot.

Shelves of wool nestled alongside boxes of buttons, stands of tapestry kits, embroidery silks, zips of all lengths, knitting needles, knitting patterns, crochet hooks, elastic, cottons, even a bale or two of material lurked, hidden, on a high shelf. As a wool and haberdashery shop, A Good Yarn was definitely stuck in the wrong century. Even as a Saturday girl years ago Katie had known that the shop was decidedly old-fashioned and Mattie hadn't done much, if anything, in the last few years to modernize it in any way.

If you believed the gossip in the magazines, knitting was all the rage these days with celebs proudly clicking their needles all over the place and rushing to join Stitch and Bitch clubs. Could she start a local version? Katie fingered a ball of white angora wool abandoned on a shelf. If she did take on the shop, she'd have to come up with something to grab people's interest.

Katie opened the door to the back stockroom. Rows of empty shelves showed that Mattie had been running stock down for some time. Would it be possible to turn it into a Stitch and Bitch club room? Keep the stock to a minimum? It was a large enough room.

Closing the door she climbed the narrow twisting stairs up to the first floor with its two empty rooms and an old-fashioned bathroom. She'd forgotten about these rooms. A possible kitchen and bedroom? Could she possibly live over the shop?

The attic that spanned the width of the building gave her the answer. The large room with its dormer windows looking out towards the two castles at the mouth of the river was dusty and empty save for a few old, battered cardboard boxes. In her mind's eye it was instantly transformed into a delightful sitting-room with comfy settees and chairs, bookshelves holding her books and CDs. Yes, she could definitely live up here.

Deep in thought, Katie made her way back downstairs. Taking over the shop would certainly solve her immediate problem of finding a job. It would help Mattie too. It could be fun to spend a summer down here; revisit some of her old haunts. She could—

Katie screamed as a pair of burly arms wrapped around her and held her tight.

'Got you. What the hell do you think you're up to?'

Relief flooded through Katie's body as she recognized the voice.

'Leo Cranford! Let me go. It's Katie.'

'Tiggy?'

If there had been any doubt in Katie's mind that her captor was Leo Cranford, his use of her childish nickname was enough to dispel it.

'I've told you – don't call me that. You know I hate it. Now let me GO.' Sharply jarring her elbows back into Leo's body she twisted herself out of his grip.

'What are you doing here?' he demanded, staring at her as she rubbed her arms where he'd gripped them.

'Never mind what I'm doing. What the hell are you playing at? Frightening me like that.'

'I saw the lights downstairs, and thought someone had broken in. You're lucky I didn't call the police.'

Deciding her best policy was to say nothing, Katie glared at him. Leo had had quite a short temper in the past.

'So, what exactly are you doing in Mattie's shop?'

'Working out whether it's a feasible business proposition.'

'For Mattie?'

'For me,' Katie said.

'You're coming back? Giving up all things meedja?'

Katie tried not to smile at Leo's deliberate usual mispronunciation of media. 'Yes.'

'But you couldn't wait to get away. Said nothing would ever drag you back down here.'

'A girl can change her mind, can't she?'

Leo regarded her thoughtfully for several seconds before holding out his hand. 'In that case – welcome home.'

Leo's farm work-hardened hand all but crushed her fingers as he took her hand in his. The final decision to return seemed to have been made the moment Leo asked if she was giving up all things media.

Leo walked back to Mattie's with Katie and gave in easily to his aunt's, 'You'll stay for supper, won't you? Help me persuade Katie to take on A Good Yarn.'

'No persuading necessary – I've decided I'll do it,' Katie said. 'Though heaven knows what I'm letting myself in for. I do have a few ideas for attracting customers but really, I know nothing about running a shop.'

'Oh, you'll soon get the hang of it,' Mattie said. 'I'll still be around to help out a bit.'

'Good. We'll work out a plan of action,' Katie said.

'After supper we'll have a brainstorming session,' Mattie said. 'Leo can give us a man's point of view.'

'Mmm,' Katie said. Remembering Leo's teenage skull and cross bones decorating phase she wasn't at all sure she wanted to hear Leo's views. 'First thing is to get the place spruced up. Lots of white paint everywhere, I think. Open plan space. New shelving units. We'll need to make the flat habitable too. I can't stay here with you forever,' she said quickly as she saw Mattie about to protest.

'I suppose not. But at least for the first couple of months,' Mattie said. 'If I go on the Mediterranean cruise I've dreamed of for years, it'd be good to have you here to look after Bert. Can't put him in kennels.'

'Think I'd better go home tomorrow,' Katie said. 'Get things organized up there. Hand the flat keys over to the agency. Say goodbye to friends.'

'Any friend in particular?' Leo asked.

'Mainly Lara and Patrick,' Katie said. How Patrick would react to her plans would be interesting. Hopefully he would be pleased for her. Before Leo could start asking questions about who Patrick was, Katie added: 'There's also a couple of factory outlets up there I'd like to take a look at – see if I can get some ideas for stock. I'll drive back down next Sunday, if that's OK with you,' she said, looking at Mattie.

'In time for tea would be good,' Mattie said.

'OK. But go easy on the clotted cream. Eat too many of your famous teas and I'll end up getting fat.'

'You, fat? Rubbish,' Leo said. 'Anyway, you could do with a bit more meat on you. You're a bit too skinny for me.'

'Oh really,' Katie said. 'Then it's just as well I'm nothing to do with you, isn't it?'

Mattie laughed. 'Listen to you two. Just like old times already. Oh, it's going to be great fun having the pair of you together again.'

After waving Katie off Monday morning, Mattie made her way down to the shop. Last night the three of them had decided she would put a notice on the door, informing everyone that the shop was closing for a short time and would re-open under new management at the end of the month. Leo had said he'd meet her down there and they would start to plan how to give the place a modern-day makeover.

Mattie looked around the shop where she'd spent so much of her life. Was she doing the right thing handing the place over to Katie? The war and Clara's death had meant she'd had no choice over accepting her own unwanted legacy. Forcing Katie to follow in her footsteps down a road in life she wasn't enthusiastic about – well, she simply couldn't do it. But Katie hadn't rejected the idea outright, had she?

A Good Yarn had been a thriving business once, surely it could be again. It just needed a modern-style management. And there was no doubt Katie would infuse the place with up-to-date ideas.

Mattie jumped as the shop doorbell jangled and Leo appeared.

'Morning. You look deep in thought,' Leo said.

'I was trying to reassure myself that I am doing the right thing by Katie,' Mattie said. 'Don't want to lumber her with a business that is beyond saving.'

'I doubt that Katie would take it on if she didn't think she could make a go of it,' Leo said. 'I'd have thought it's got lots of potential. The idea of starting a Stitch and Bitch club is a good one too.'

Mattie winced as the noise of banging and shouting from next door resonated through the shop.

'Seems like the developers are back. Been quiet in there for months. Must have got an injection of cash,' she said. 'Hope they don't cause too much disruption but it'd be good to see the Old Salt House get a lick of paint. Even if it is being turned into yet more flats. Right – ideas for this place?"

'Katie mentioned lots of white paint and an open-plan space,' Leo said.

'Think that old dresser could do with pulling out,' Mattie said.

Part open shelves and part glass cupboard, it completely filled the wall behind the counter. 'It's been there forever. Maybe now is the time to take it out? Put something more modern in.'

Leo shook his head as he moved behind the counter. 'Got to disagree there. This distressed dresser is perfect as it is.'

Mattie looked at him. 'Distressed? Don't know about that. It looks downright miserable to me and in need of a good coat of paint – or burning.'

'Trust me on this one. It'll be fine. A modern fashion statement. Think that utility unit over there needs to come out though. What's this?' Leo bent down and gently pulled at a photograph trapped between the wooden shelves of the bottom dresser cupboard. Closing the dresser door he handed a faded, grainy, black and white photograph to Mattie.

A boyish-looking man in uniform, his arm around the shoulders of a pretty young woman, was laughing at the camera, while a young girl clung to his back, her arms flung tight around his neck in a determined effort not to fall off.

'Isn't that you with Aunt Clara and her American boyfriend during the war?' Leo asked. 'You all look as though you were having fun.'

'Oh, we were,' Mattie said. She handed the photo back for Leo to have a closer look.

It had been such a happy day. Gallants Bower out by the castle had recently been classified as out of bounds to the locals but Hal had sneaked them through for a picnic in the woods.

He'd even brought candies and a bottle of lemonade. Sworn to secrecy Mattie had never told anyone about that afternoon when, for a couple of hours, the small corner of her world had been such a happy place.

The row that broke out two nights later between Clara and their parents was a bitter one, ending with Clara being forbidden to see Hal ever again. From then on not only was there war with Germany, there was full-out war between Clara and their parents.

Nobody explained to Mattie what the row was about. Even Clara had wearily responded with the usual, 'You're just a child; you wouldn't understand. I'll explain one day when you're older.'

But that day had never arrived. Instead Operation Tiger had happened in Start Bay and the light went out of Clara's eyes before she left home, never to return.

Leo gently tapped Mattie on the shoulder and gave her the photo back. 'You OK?'

Mattie nodded. 'Yes. Just remembering and wishing things could have turned out differently for Clara. I'll pop this in with the family photos when I get home.'

'Now, what are we going to do to surprise Katie?' Leo said and the two of them spent the rest of the day preparing the shop for its makeover.

Tired when she reached home that evening, Mattie made herself manhandle the loft ladder down before climbing up into the attic. If she didn't put the picture in a safe place straight away she might lose it.

She pulled the box containing all that remained of Clara's

belongings from under the eaves and took it downstairs. She rarely opened the box these days, the memories it stirred were still too painful. Taking the lid off, the remembered miscellaneous collection of things met her gaze.

A few photos, a couple of paperbacks, ornaments, a silver-backed hairbrush, a passport, a ration book, some old school notebooks, bits of jewellery and a 1943 guide to American towns. A sealed A4-sized envelope lined the bottom of the box.

How her parents had selected such a random collection of items as a memento of their elder daughter's life was beyond comprehension. What criteria had they used? The only truly personal item in the box was Clara's hairbrush.

Mattie brushed a tear away. Forbidden by her parents to ever mention Clara's name to them again, she'd cried herself to sleep night after night. From the day she'd learnt of Clara's death she'd masked her feelings about her sister from everyone. It had been easier that way and now it was too late to change.

Mattie took the photograph out of her bag. 'Oh, Clara,' she said, gently stroking the image of her sister's face. 'The past is past but I so wish you'd had a future too. We both deserved so much more.'

With one last look she carefully placed the photo in the box along with the others before closing it again and pushing the box underneath her bed. It could stay there for a while. She was too tired to climb up into the loft to put it away.

TWO

'A wool shop? That's for grannies. You're too young to bury yourself in the country. What's happened to your career plans?' Patrick ran his hands through his dark, foppishly cut hair. 'I can't believe you're serious about this.'

'Redundancy happened,' Katie said. 'Perhaps a change of direction is what I need. Besides, Mattie needs me. I'm doing this for her as much as me.'

Patrick shook his head in disbelief. 'Because some old woman has played on your conscience you're going home to run a doomed business.'

'Mattie is my godmother – not some old woman,' Katie snapped. Whatever reaction she'd expected from Patrick it wasn't this rhetoric against Mattie. 'She didn't play on my conscience. We've agreed I'll give it a year and if it doesn't work out, A Good Yarn will be sold.'

'What about us? When are we going to see each other?'

'I'll only be two hours down the motorway – one and a half, the way you drive,' Katie said. 'You can come for long weekends once I'm settled in the flat.'

'That's something else – I thought we could look for a new place for the two of us up here in Clifton. Finally move in together, show the world we're a couple. But now we're breaking up.'

'Patrick, we are not breaking up – unless that's what you want to happen. I'm just going to be working away but I'll be popping back from time to time. Anyway, without a job there's no way I can afford to contribute to a new place.'

'Still sounds like the death knell to our relationship, to me,' Patrick said. 'Well, I'm warning you – don't expect me to stay in and meditate. I shall still have a social life with or without you.'

'I expect you will,' Katie said. 'So shall I when I'm not working. I've got lots of friends down there still,' she added, her fingers crossed behind her back.

Well, Lara and Dexter would be down sometime in the summer. Most of her other friends had, like her, left to find work and rarely returned. Anyway she'd be too busy with the shop to bother about much of a social life in the beginning.

In the end Patrick had thrown up his hands in despair. 'I give you six months at the most before you're bored out of your mind and back up here looking for a job.'

When Katie phoned Lara to tell her about Patrick's attitude, Lara had reacted with her typical bluntness.

'What d'you expect from a selfish prick like him? He's not thinking about you – just how inconvenient it will be for him when you leave.'

'Don't hold back, will you?' Katie protested.

'You know I've never liked Patrick,' Lara said. 'I think it's great you're ditching him and going back to live in Devon.'

'I'm not ditching him. He's going to come and see me when I'm settled in the flat.'

'Well, you'll never get a better opportunity to ditch him. New start. New boyfriend. Perfect.'

It was Patrick's words, though, that were ringing in Katie's head as she drove down to Devon on Sunday afternoon. Did she have totally unrealistic hopes for this new life of hers? Was she making a huge mistake? Would she find herself failing and returning up country to try to re-establish a career in the media? She could imagine how many times Patrick would delight in saying, 'Told you so'.

She'd hoped they would have had supper together last night but Patrick had claimed he was too busy. He'd finally wished her all the luck in the world. 'Because boy, are you going to need it.'

Driving down College Way and seeing the river dazzle in the afternoon sunlight, Katie pushed all thoughts of Patrick and his gloomy predictions out of her mind. This afternoon it felt good to be coming home. She'd make things work out.

To her surprise Leo was waiting for her at the shop. The strong smell of fresh paint hit her as she walked in.

'Mattie organized a cleaner. You'd already said you wanted open plan and lots of white paint everywhere, so I thought I'd give you a head start.'

'Gosh, Leo. I've only been gone six days,' Katie said. 'You must have lived here to get all this done in that time. I owe you.'

Leo shrugged. 'Come on, let's get your stuff in. Where d'you want it put?'

'Oh, let's just dump it in the stockroom,' Katie said. 'I can sort it out from there. I'm sure you need to get back to the farm.'

Leo shook his head. 'No. Life's a lot easier since I stopped milking. Not such a rigid structure to the day with sheep. Besides, I'm invited to join you at Mattie's for tea.'

Between them, Katie's possessions were soon stacking up on the stockroom floor.

'What are you doing with your car?' Leo asked as he carried the last of the boxes in. 'Yellow lines everywhere. No parking up at Mattie's at all.'

'Hadn't thought about that,' Katie said. 'I guess it'll be the main car park. I'll have to organize a season ticket.'

'Doubt you'll be using the car much,' Leo said. 'Reckon it'll be safer up in one of my barns. Come on. We'll take it up and walk back to Mattie's. You remember the way?'

'Of course I remember the way. I grew up down here, remember. And I've been back lots of times to see Mum and Dad before they went to Spain.'

'Christmas and the occasional week in summer hardly count in my book.'

'I was a working girl. I had a life away from here,' Katie said. Leo's attitude to her leaving home and doing a media course at college had always been disapproving – and annoyed her now as much as it always had.

'And now you're back. Incidentally, you've just missed the Newcomen Road turn. You'll have to go round the one-way system now.'

Driving out of town up Weeke Hill towards Leo's farm, Katie remembered the fight Leo had faced to convince his family he wanted to be a farmer and not run the family boat business. Michael, his father, had been incensed that Leo had no intention of following the family tradition and becoming a river pilot. Harsh words had been said, disinheritance threatened, but Leo had been adamant. He wanted to be a farmer and a farmer he would be.

Mattie had told her these days Castle Farm was a thriving concern, Leo's younger brother Josh was the river pilot and family squabbles had been buried.

'You did your own thing as much as I did,' Katie said. 'Only you stayed put to do it – apart from going to agricultural college.'

'True,' Leo acknowledged. 'But then I could never imagine living anywhere else. Still can't.'

'Oh, aren't the primroses beautiful,' Katie said as she turned on to the farm track and saw the carpet of dainty yellow heads lining the bank. 'My favourite flower. They've always reminded me of down here.'

'If you make for the far barn,' Leo said, 'I'll open the doors and you can drive straight in. Look out for Meg – she's a bit deaf these days.'

Once she'd parked alongside a gleaming green tractor, Katie wandered out to the farmyard to wait as Leo closed and padlocked the barn doors. Near the duck pond in front of the farmhouse, Katie bent down to stroke Meg, Leo's old collie, who greeted her with much tail-wagging.

The old granite farmhouse, with its mullioned windows and ivy-covered walls nestling in a dip in the hillside, was in sharp contrast to the modern outbuildings around the farmyard that had replaced the original derelict sheds and pigsties she remembered.

'It must be five years since I've been up here,' Katie said when Leo joined her. 'You've certainly improved things out here. What about the house? You still camping out?' she teased, remembering how shocked she'd been the last time she'd been in the house.

Leo had been too busy getting the farm to work, he'd said, to do anything about the old house. It was there to simply provide a roof over his head in between his labours.

'Take a look around,' he said now, pushing open the heavy oak front door. 'I need to change out of these clothes. Can't go to Mattie's reeking of turps.'

The kitchen Katie remembered, with its chipped stone sink, camping stove and tatty armchair, was no more. Walls had been knocked down, windows realigned, a stable door added. A large scarlet Aga stood in the old inglenook, its gentle heat an invitation to linger nearby. Katie placed a hand on the warm lid, wondering what sort of meals Leo cooked these days. It would be a waste, she thought, not to use this cooker.

'I make a mean lasagne,' Leo said, reappearing in black jeans and a black polo shirt and seemingly reading her thoughts. 'You must try it one evening. Right now though, it's time to get back to Mattie's.' Leo took some keys off a board by the door.

'Be quicker if we take the bike – fancy riding pillion? Or are you too sophisticated these days?'

Katie glared at him. 'Fine – so long as you've lost your desire to die young by doing stupid things like wheelies at sixty miles an hour with me on the back.'

Leo grinned. 'That was a fun ride, wasn't it! No, these days I use the bike mainly to get to fire-shout call-outs.

Retained fireman,' he added, seeing Katie's blank look. 'Doing my bit.'

The flashy BMW motorbike Leo switched on before handing her a helmet and inviting her to 'Jump on, then' was far removed from the ancient bike he had loved in his teens. This one was definitely made for speed.

Katie hesitated before swinging herself onto the pillion, putting her arms around Leo's waist, closing her eyes and waiting for the inevitable noise and rush of speed. By the time she opened her eyes, the bend at Warfleet was approaching fast, so she promptly closed them again and tightened her grip around Leo's waist.

Katie's every waking moment for the next two weeks involved the shop. She finished the decorating Leo had started, assembled new display shelves, met with suppliers and talked to Mattie about her plans.

'Need some crafty things to appeal to holidaymakers – local pottery, paintings of local scenes, that kind of thing. Know of any local artists?' she asked.

'Woman in Brixham makes felt bags,' Mattie replied. 'And my neighbour makes beautiful shell and pebble jewellery. There's a couple of local artists too who would probably appreciate some extra gallery space.'

'Great. I've ordered some tapestry sets, candle-making kits and some fun kits for the kids to try. Thought I'd start a Knit, Stitch and Listen book club in the back room too, rather than a Stitch and Bitch. Think they're a bit passé now. A sort of crafty book club. I could sell stuff the members make if it's good enough.'

'You could hold the occasional workshop,' Mattie said thoughtfully.

'That's an idea. Fancy teaching an Aran knitting class? I've still got the sweater you made me before I went off to uni.'

'After my holiday maybe,' Mattie said. 'Which reminds me – I've got an appointment with the travel agent. Can I leave Bert with you for half an hour?'

'Sure. We'll walk to the travel agents with you and then I'll give him a run in the park. I need some exercise and fresh air,' Katie said.

Leaving Mattie at the travel agents, Katie walked through Avenue Gardens towards the North Embankment. Holding Bert's lead firmly, she stopped to watch the Higher Ferry disgorge its latest load of passengers.

A scarlet, low-slung sports car, carefully negotiating the bump between the wooden ferry ramp and the concrete terra firma slope, reminded her of Patrick and his beloved classic Morgan car. He'd have been totally paranoid about dragging the exhaust of his precious car on the ramp.

Patrick. Was he missing her? Doubtful – she hadn't heard from him since she left. Not a text, an email or a phone call to even check she'd arrived safely. He always could sulk for England. Maybe he was waiting for her to offer the proverbial olive branch?

Taking her mobile out, she typed: 'Hi. U OK? Evrthg gd hr. Ms u. L K8.' She pressed send and waited, anticipating an immediate reply. Zilch. Her phone remained stubbornly silent. Oh, well. She'd tried.

When she and Bert returned from their walk Leo was

outside the shop having a heated discussion with an elderly man. As she approached, the man glowered at her before muttering to Leo, 'Mark my words; this isn't the last of it. Family's family. Blood should be thicker than water.' With a spiteful look in Katie's direction, he marched off towards the Lower Ferry.

'Who's that?'

'Ron from Blackawton,' Leo said.

'Didn't look too happy,' Katie said. 'Oh, is he the one Mattie mentioned wanting to get his hands on the shop?'

'That's him. Don't worry about him. He's all wind.' Leo glanced at Katie. 'All the same we won't mention this to Mattie, all right, little Tiggy? No point in upsetting her.'

Katie nodded, too concerned about Ron to react to Leo's use of her childish nickname again.

Leo followed Katie back into the shop and stayed to help her prepare the stockroom ready for painting and its makeover into a friendly clubroom.

'You still thinking about living upstairs?'

'Definitely,' Katie nodded. 'Though Mattie is insisting I stay with her until after her holiday at least. Think she just wants to make sure I'm around for Bert while she's away,' she added, looking at the dog sleeping on the mat by the door.

'Let me know when you're ready to make a start up there and I'll give you a hand,' Leo offered.

'Will do. Thanks.' Katie glanced at him. 'You coming to the grand opening at the weekend?'

'Wouldn't miss it for the world,' Leo grinned at her. 'Little Tiggy coming home to run a shop – who'd have thought it?'

Katie glared at him. 'It's Katie – and what's so funny about me running a shop?'

'Nothing. It just seems an unlikely thing for the Katie I knew to be doing, that's all.'

Resisting the urge to throw something at him – he was helping her after all – Katie said, 'I'm doing it for Mattie as much as me. I think she's looking very tired these days.'

'She's perked up a lot since you've come back. She likes having you around. Where d'you want these boxes put?'

'Attic room, please. It'll be the last room to be done.'

THREE

Four days later, Katie and Mattie were doing last minute fitting out and shelf-stocking before the grand reopening of A Good Yarn, which Katie had planned for Saturday morning. The shop was pristine and colourful, filled with skeins of wool, books of knitting patterns, sewing kits, button cabinets, embroidery silks, tapestry sets and other hobby crafts.

One wall was devoted to 'Local Crafts' and those shelves held an assortment of pottery, candles, jewellery and other handmade stuff. Seascape paintings by a friend of Mattie's were dotted around in gaps on the walls, discreet stickers showing their prices. A rack of local postcards stood ready to be pushed outside.

The old stockroom had been transformed – with the help of some furniture from Mattie – into a comfy, inviting room with easy chairs, a table with a sewing machine, a bookcase, a CD player, coffee machine and china mugs in the corner – all ready for the first meeting of the Knit, Stitch and Listen book club next week.

'Oh, these are fun,' Mattie said, unpacking a box of knitted flowers. 'Where shall I put them?'

'Some on the counter by the till,' Katie said, handing her a wicker basket to place a selection in. 'The rest can go on the shelf with the other decorative stuff.'

'You going to wear one tomorrow? Showcase the goods and all that?'

'Definitely. You must wear one too.'

'D'you think we could persuade Leo to wear one?' Mattie laughed. 'You'd never have managed all this without him and his muscles.'

'I owe him, big time,' Katie said seriously. 'But I doubt I can persuade him to wear a knitted flower.' She glanced at Mattie. 'Always thought he'd be married by now with a family running around the farmhouse.'

'He tells me he's been too busy setting the farm up and getting the house habitable,' Mattie said. 'Guess he'll get around to it soon. May I have this cream rose?'

Bert, stretched out in what had become his usual position on the mat by the front door, barked as an envelope was pushed through the letter box and landed on his back. Katie picked it up and examined it curiously. Finding it addressed to 'The Owner, A Good Yarn', she automatically held it out to Mattie.

Mattie shook her head. 'That's you now. You open it.'

'There's going to be an American film company in town soon, making a documentary about life down here during World War II. They're promising to keep the disruption to the minimum and,' Katie looked up at Mattie, 'they're keen to find people to talk to who lived here then.'

'Well, they needn't look at me,' Mattie said. 'I was only a child. They wouldn't be interested in my memories.'

'Why not? The few things you've told me about the town then are fascinating – all that business where everyone was evacuated from around here, Operation Overlord. That American – Clara's boyfriend – showing you how to play basketball. Coronation Park being out of bounds.'

'Ancient history. They should let it be,' Mattie said. 'It does no good at all raking it up all the time. When are they coming?'

'Next week to do some more research and start filming. They're reckoning on being in town for most of the summer,' Katie said.

'At least I'll be away for some of the time,' Mattie said. 'Right, what's in this last packet?'

'Poster and leaflets advertising the club,' Katie said. 'I'll stick the poster up on the door and leave a pile on the counter ready to hand out tomorrow.'

'Knit, Stitch and Listen book club. Tuesday evenings and Thursday afternoons. Join for a couple of hours' creative fun and listen to the latest bestseller,' Mattie read. 'Is Christopher organizing the audio books for you?'

'Yes, and a few paperbacks too. I just hope people find the idea of the club a good one and we get some members.'

Katie made her way to the shop early Saturday morning. She needed to get a head start decorating the doors and windows with balloons, banners and ribbons. She was determined that the shop would look festive for the opening ceremony later.

The caterers had promised to deliver the champagne, nibbles and a cake at 10.30. Mattie, as the VIP guest, would cut the red ribbon strung across the entrance as she declared A Good Yarn once again open for business.

Katie stood stock-still as the shop came into view. What the hell had happened overnight? White paint obliterated both windows. The glass panel of the front door had been smashed. There was glass everywhere. A policeman was standing in the entrance writing in his notebook.

'What's going on?'

'Seems somebody went on the rampage. You the owner?'

Katie nodded.

'You'd better check out the inside. See if anything obvious is missing – but don't touch things in case the forensic boys need to come.'

Rather than simply stepping through the hole, Katie unlocked the door and crunched over the broken glass. Inside, everything appeared to be as she and Mattie had left it last night. Nothing disturbed. Nothing missing.

'Looks like plain vandalism rather than burglary, then,' the police officer said.

'But only me targeted,' Katie said, looking at the empty buildings next door and the shops across the narrow street. 'Why?'

'You're the nearest to the pub. Drunken louts, I expect. I'll have a word with the landlord. See if he had any trouble last night. Might be worth you investing in some steel shutters for the windows and door. Stop it happening again.'

Katie rang Mattie. 'We have a problem,' she said. 'It's going to take time to clear things up. Might have to postpone the grand opening.'

'Nonsense. I'll get Leo. He'll soon have the place sorted.'

Katie sighed as she fetched a broom and began to sweep up the glass. Impromptu drunken vandalism didn't explain the white paint daubed all over the place. Was someone out to stop her before she'd even started?

Leo abandoned his bike on Bayards Cove and gave her a tight hug when he arrived ten minutes later. 'Don't worry, Tiggy. We'll soon have the place back to normal. I've phoned a mate to come and replace the glass in the door.'

'There's a bottle of paint stripper out back,' he said. 'I'll make a start on cleaning the windows.'

'Police got any idea who's responsible?' he asked.

'Probably drunks. But drunks wouldn't have had tins of paint on them, would they?'

Leo grunted, stretching to reach some paint high on the window. 'Kids often carry aerosols ready for a spot of graffiti. Don't worry. This place will be as good as new in time for the opening.'

Katie hesitated, not wanting to put the thought into words. 'You don't think it's Ron the Blackawton cousin making his feelings known?'

Leo shook his head. 'No. Like I said – that one is all wind. Reckon the police have it right. Drunken louts.'

'Hope you're right,' Katie sighed.

'Sure I am Tig . . . Katie. Got the coffee on yet? Missed my normal breakfast cup, racing down here. Black, no sugar.'

When she got back with his coffee Leo had finished one window and was busy on the other one. His friend had arrived and was efficiently measuring the door for replacement glass, which he promised would be in situ within the hour.

The place was already beginning to look better. Leo was right. Things would be back to normal in time for the opening. Katie's heartbeat slowed and she began to relax.

Once the windows were clean and the door repaired, Leo climbed the ladder and pinned the 'Grand Reopening' banner across the front of the building. Together they blew up and then hung bunches of balloons from the upstairs windows. The red ribbon was tacked onto one side of the entrance ready to be tied across the doorway prior to Mattie's speech and the cutting ceremony.

The caterers arrived with the champagne and the nibbles. In amongst the usual junk mail and bills the postman delivered several good luck cards, including one from Patrick. She'd sent him an email to tell him the date of the opening ceremony but he hadn't replied.

Katie laughed out loud as she saw the flying pink pig illustration. Patrick's message, though – 'Hope these aren't flying past your place in the future. Good luck. Patrick' – made her sigh. She hoped so too. She'd ring him later. Tell him how things went.

With half an hour to go, Leo disappeared in a roar of exhaust noise to go back to the farm, change his clothes and to collect Mattie.

The florist turned up with two bouquets. About to protest she'd only ordered the lily one for presenting to Mattie as a thank-you gesture, Katie saw the second one, yellow and cream roses, was addressed to her from Leo.

'Welcome back, Tiggy, and good luck. Leo.'

Katie put the card in her pocket before hiding Mattie's bouquet out of sight and placing the basket of roses on the counter where they started to fill the shop with their wonderful scent.

'Miss Teague?'

Katie turned. 'Yes?'

'Dave – reporter from the *Chronicle*. Can I take a photo of you working here in the shop before the ceremony? I gather you had a spot of bother here this morning. Likely to delay the opening?'

'No. Everything is back to normal now,' Katie said, self-consciously standing where Dave indicated by the counter as he clicked away. 'Should all start to happen in about five minutes when my VIP guest arrives. So if you'll excuse me, I still have to get the ribbon tied across the door. And to find the scissors.'

Katie, fixing the red ribbon across the door, heard a childish voice calling out, 'Atie, Atie. We're a surprise!'

'What a surprise,' Katie said, turning and seeing Lara and Dexter and their daughter Daisy laughing at her. 'Haven't learnt to say your Ks yet then, Daisy,' she said, picking up the little girl and cuddling her.

'What are you doing here?' she said, looking at Lara and Dexter. 'How long are you down for?'

'Couldn't miss the grand opening. We leave after lunch tomorrow,' Lara said. 'So we've got this evening to catch up.'

Leo and Mattie arrived at that moment with Bert, a red scarf tied around his neck, straining on his lead. Mattie laughingly acknowledged the good-natured cheers of the small crowd that had gathered.

Katie watched as Mattie greeted various friends – Christopher from the bookshop, Luke, the owner of one of the nearby restaurants, and Pete – 'fishing trips rounds the bay' – before Leo escorted her to the beribboned entrance.

'Right,' Mattie said. 'To business. You hold Bert and give me the scissors.'

Smiling, Katie took charge of Bert and handed the scissors over.

'I declare A Good Yarn well and truly open for business and wish Katie every success. Ta-da!' Mattie said, cutting the ribbon with a flourish. 'The champagne is on the house. Now, where's Bert?'

'He's here,' Katie said. 'But hang on two secs....' She gave Mattie a quick hug before fetching the bouquet. 'Thank you for trusting me with A Good Yarn. I promise not to let you down.' She handed Mattie the lilies, giving her another quick hug in the process.

Leo appeared at her side with a glass of champagne.

'Thanks for the roses. They're beautiful,' Katie said.

Leo's brown eyes were serious as they clinked glasses. 'Pleased to have you back in town, Tiggy. Here's to the future. I'm sure A Good Yarn will be a huge success in your hands.'

'Hope so,' Katie said, looking at Mattie and everyone milling around. There were so many people wishing her well and Mattie was relying on her. What the hell was she thinking taking on a wool shop? She was a film production manager, for God's sake.

'You'll be Businesswoman of the Year before you know it,' Lara said, appearing at her side. 'So stop worrying.'

Katie laughed. Lara had always had this uncanny knack of second-guessing her feelings.

'Hope you're right. Not that I particularly want to be Businesswoman of the Year – I just want the shop to be successful.'

'And it will be. Now, Dexter and I have to get back to the boatyard for the afternoon, Daisy is desperate to play with her cousins, but we're invited to Leo's for supper this evening. We'll pick you up on our way. About 7.30, OK?'

The queue beginning to form at the counter caught Katie's attention. 'OK. See you later,' she said, moving towards the queue. Mattie was staring, frustrated, at the new electronic till which Katie had bought to replace the old National cash register with its dodgy keys and temperamental cash drawer that had been in the shop since before the war. It could only be a matter of seconds before Mattie attempted to bash the innovation into submission.

Thanks to the champagne which Leo had insisted they needed to toast 'the newest shopkeeper in town', there was a party atmosphere around the big wooden table in his farmhouse kitchen later that evening.

Candles and the light from a couple of old-fashioned oil lamps were casting a soft glow over the room. Leo had cooked honey-roast lamb with rosemary, roast potatoes and asparagus, followed by apple crumble and clotted cream.

'Didn't realise you were such a good cook these days,' Katie said. 'Takeaway pizza used to be your idea of a good meal.'

'Can you please give Dexter a few tips,' Lara said. 'He's hopeless in the kitchen. If he can't open a ready-prepared meal he's lost. It's all those years living on shipboard rations.'

'I have other talents,' Dexter said quietly. 'Have you told Katie our news yet?'

'Told me what? Oh,' Katie said, interpreting the look that passed between Lara and Dexter. 'Daisy's going to have company? I wondered why you weren't swigging the champagne down. Congratulations.'

'Early days yet, but yes,' Lara said.

'More champagne needed, I think,' Leo said, 'to toast that news. Although not for you, obviously, Lara!'

'In that case I'll have the last helping of apple crumble. Pass the cream, please.'

As Katie stood up to clear the table, Leo turned to Dexter. 'Want to see my new silage cutter? Got it earlier this week.' The two men disappeared out into the farmyard.

'That is so typical of farmers,' Lara laughed. 'Surprised Leo didn't start singing *I've got a Brand New Combine Harvester*.'

'I'm so glad you came for the opening,' Katie said. 'Wouldn't have been the same without you here.' The whole day had been brilliant – apart from the vandalism – and this evening with two of her oldest friends and Dexter had been good too. Totally relaxed and casual – just the way she'd used to spend her evenings. Which meant of course that Patrick would have hated everything. Spending a Saturday evening in a farmhouse was definitely not his scene.

'Thought Patrick might have done the decent thing and shown up today,' Lara said, stacking plates in the dishwasher. 'Or at least phoned?'

'He hasn't forgiven me yet for taking on the shop. He did send a card wishing me luck but other than that,' she shrugged, 'I haven't heard a peep from him.'

'Good. Hopefully he's got the message you've ditched him.'

'Why do you keep on about me ditching him?' Katie demanded. 'I haven't.'

'Because he's all wrong for you. Trust me – I'm happily married and I know these things!'

'I know you've never made any real attempt to get to know him. That time we all went out to the concert together was a disaster – you were so rude to him.' Should she tell Lara what Patrick had said afterwards about Lara having attitude?

'Well, that should have told you something. Besides, I was only rude in retaliation. He started it first.'

'Who exactly is this Patrick?'

Both Katie and Lara turned at the sound of Leo's voice. Neither had heard him return to the kitchen.

'My boyfriend,' Katie said, deciding there was no reason why she shouldn't tell Leo about Patrick. After all if – no, when – Patrick came for a visit, the two men would undoubtedly meet, so it was best if Leo knew about him now.

Leo picked up a catalogue from the dresser. 'Not a very supportive boyfriend by the sounds of it. Maybe he's ditched you, rather than wait for you to dump him,' he said, before opening the kitchen door. 'Anyway, long distance relationships rarely work.' The door closed behind him, leaving Katie staring after him open-mouthed.

'What the hell does he know about long distance relationships anyway?' Katie said, turning to Lara. 'It's not as if he's ever had one. That is so typical of Leo to jump to the wrong conclusion.'

'He was seeing someone up country when he came back

from agriculture college,' Lara said. 'Told Dexter it only lasted a few months once he was home.'

'I didn't know that,' Katie said. 'OK, maybe he's had a bad experience and absence didn't make his heart grow fonder but Patrick and I are different. Once I've got the flat sorted, he'll be down regularly at weekends – and I'll go up there too.'

Lara shrugged. 'Still think you're making a mistake. Personally I hope Patrick has taken the coward's way out and dumped you without telling you.'

Katie shook her head. 'No. I know Patrick isn't like that. He'd tell me.'

FOUR

The following morning, Katie took Bert and walked up to Castle Farm to fetch her car. After the previous night's set-to with Leo, she couldn't help wondering what sort of reception she was going to get from him.

She'd left with Lara and Dexter last night shortly after Leo had given her his opinion of long distance relationships. One word about Patrick this morning and she'd tell him to butt out and mind his own business.

Leo was moving hay bales in the small barn as Katie arrived on the farmyard.

'Give you a hand with those?' she offered, standing in the barn entrance.

'Thanks,' Leo said. 'Not sure a townie like you will have the strength, though,' he added, grinning at her as he effortlessly threw a bale onto a trailer.

Katie picked one up and threw it towards the trailer. Not for the world would she have told Leo her feelings of relief when, a mere half a dozen bales later, he called a halt.

'Trailer's up to capacity now, thanks. Glass of water?'

Standing in the kitchen and handing her a welcome glass

of water, Leo asked, 'So what are you doing up here this morning anyway?'

'I've come to collect my car and to invite you to join Mattie and me for lunch in Torcross,' Katie said. 'I meant to ask you last night but I forgot.' Which was a bit of a white lie. She'd deliberately chosen not to mention Sunday lunch to him because she was so cross with him. This morning she'd calmed down and decided to ask him after all.

'My treat, as a small thank-you for all your help,' she said.

Leo shook his head. 'Sorry, no can do. Already got plans for lunch. Another day?' He reached across and picked her car keys off the keyboard. 'You'll need these. Drive carefully.'

'Thanks. Another time, then,' Katie said. Why wasn't she surprised Leo already had plans for lunch? He'd always had a well-established social life with lots of mates even before she'd left home. Clearly nothing had changed.

Half an hour later, she and Mattie were driving along the coastal road that led to Torcross. Parking in the car park, Katie glanced at the small crowd of men clustered around an old black army tank.

'That army tank has become a real tourist attraction hasn't it?' she said.

'Oh, there's always some American poking around it. Can't see the attraction myself. Should have left it at the bottom of Start Bay,' Mattie said dismissively. 'Shall we go straight to the restaurant?'

Without waiting for an answer she sped across the road to the annoyance of an oncoming car driver, who was forced to slow down and vented his anger with a loud blast of his horn.

Katie shook her head at Mattie when she finally caught up with her. 'Carry on like that and you won't make many more lunches.'

'I just do not understand the obsession men have with war and war machines,' Mattie said. 'It's so misplaced. The effects of the destruction and the life-shattering changes that happen to ordinary people continue long after the war itself finishes.'

'But we should never forget, should we?' Katie asked quietly.

'No, of course not. I never will.' Mattie was silent for a moment before sighing. 'If it hadn't been for all the events involving that tank, Clara's life – and ultimately mine – would have been so different. It's impossible to change history so the best thing to do is to let it go. No point at all dwelling on the past and what might have been. Lunch?'

Thinking about Mattie's words, Katie followed her into the restaurant. Mattie had always been reluctant to talk about the past and she'd never known her to talk about Clara in any detail, but clearly she had some bottled-up, unhappy and disturbing memories of her early life.

Katie tried several times over lunch to get Mattie to tell her more about her childhood but Mattie kept the conversation firmly on her plans for booking a holiday and how much she was looking forward to going away for the first time in years.

'With you looking after Bert, I don't have to worry about him. Such a relief,' she said.

'Talking about Bert, we'd better make a move and go home

to let him out,' Katie said. 'You sure about walking back down from Leo's? I can drop you off home and take the car back on my own, no problem.'

'I'm looking forward to the walk,' Mattie said.

As Katie drove into the farmyard, Leo was talking to a woman in a white car parked in front of the house.

'Katie, you remember Emma Pine,' Leo said when Katie walked over to give him the keys, after parking her car in the barn.

'Yes of course. Glad to see you again, Emma,' Katie said.

'You too,' Emma replied. 'Leo's been telling me all about your plans. I hope it all works out for you.'

'Thank you,' Katie said. Was Emma the *'I've already made plans for lunch'* Leo had told her about? If she was, why did she feel so resentful? It was nothing to do with her who Leo had lunch with.

'Afraid I've got to go,' Emma said. 'I'll pop into the shop soon and we'll catch up. See you Wednesday evening, Leo,' and blowing a kiss in Leo's direction, she drove off.

'Good girl, that Emma,' Mattie said as they started to walk back down to town. 'She'd make an ideal farmer's wife and it's about time Leo settled down.'

The meeting with Emma, and Mattie's comments, had somehow put a dampener on the day for Katie. The high adrenalin of the previous weeks and the excitement of opening the shop was calming down. Tomorrow, A Good Yarn would be open full-time for business and life would take on a more normal routine. A social life would become possible ... after she'd decorated the flat.

Once that was habitable, she'd invite Patrick down for a

visit. Would he come, though? He hadn't bothered phoning to see how yesterday had gone – he couldn't still be sulking, could he?

While Mattie was sorting Bert's evening meal, Katie wandered into the garden with her mobile. She'd ring Patrick and tell him about yesterday, how well it had all gone. He was usually home on Sunday evening. So what if he thought she was needy. Right at this moment she was.

'Hi,' she said. 'How are you?'

'Fine. You?'

'I'm fine too. Thanks for the card. Wish you could have been here, though.'

'Simply not possible. And I'm too busy to chat for long now. Got a meeting with a big new client tomorrow – lots of preparation to do this evening. The agency could break into the real big-time with this.'

'Exciting. Any details you can tell me?'

'Afraid not. It's all hush hush until it's announced. Katie, I've really got to go. A friend's just arrived. See you.'

'See you,' Katie echoed and ended the call. It didn't seem as though Patrick was missing her one little bit. He hadn't even asked how her big opening day had gone, or told her who the friend was.

Maybe Leo was right – Patrick was ditching her without bothering to mention the fact to her. Drifting apart would be easier for him than a face-to-face 'It's over' conversation.

The shop was filled with the scent from Leo's roses as Katie opened the door on Monday morning and prepared for her first week of business. There were few customers around for the first hour so she concentrated on doing an eye-catching display on the shelves behind the counter.

Mattie had arrived with lunchtime sandwiches and was preparing to man the counter while Katie had a short break, when the shop door opened and a tall young man entered.

'Good-day, ladies. I'm Noah Emprey Junior, part of the film crew in town making the documentary. Just wanted to warn you, we'll be filming in Bayards Cove tomorrow. I promise we'll do our best to keep disruption to a minimum.'

Mattie ignored Noah's outstretched hand and muttered something about going to the clubroom and disappeared. Katie stared after her in surprise. Mattie was usually so well-mannered.

'Hi. Nice to meet you. I'm sorry about my godmother, it seems she's got a definite aversion to Americans,' Katie said.

Noah brushed her apology aside. 'No worries. You are?'

'Katie. Katie Teague.'

'We're looking for people willing to talk about Operation Overlord and Tiger,' Noah said. 'Don't suppose you can point me in the direction of any locals willing to talk? Your godmother?'

Katie shook her head. 'Afraid not. Mattie was only a child then and insists what she remembers is of no interest.'

'Shame.'

'Local History Society?' Katie suggested.

'Scoured their files already. What we desperately need are some personal memories. We're going out to Strete tomorrow to see a woman called Beatie. Her family were evacuated in 1943 and my father is hopeful she'll come up with some new leads.'

'Good luck. Oh, maybe you should talk to Michael, Mattie's elder brother. He used to be the river pilot – took over from his father. He might have some contacts or be prepared to talk to you.'

FIVE

At 7.30 on Tuesday evening, Katie and Mattie were in the newly furnished clubroom. Nervously, Katie fiddled and rearranged things, wondering how many – if any – people would turn up for this first meeting.

The shop door pinged.

'There you are,' Mattie said. 'Told you somebody would come.'

A teenage girl was standing by the counter, clutching a large carrier-bag. 'This where the craft club is? 'Cos I wanna join.'

'Great. I'm Katie. You're?'

'Trisha.'

'Mattie, we have our first member.'

Within a quarter of an hour the club had seven members and Katie was explaining how she hoped the club would work.

'Membership is free. All I ask is that you register, which will entitle you to 5% discount in the shop. Please feel free to come and use the room, the machines, have a coffee anytime, but Tuesday evenings will be the time we all get together and listen to a book while we work. If you can each suggest a book, I'll get Christopher to order an audio copy ready for next week.'

'Jilly Cooper's *Jump*,' Trisha said, looking around as if she expected an argument.

'How will we decide the order to read in?' demanded a large woman already busy clicking away with a pair of knitting needles and a ball of grey wool. 'Should be a joint decision.'

'How about we put all the suggestions in a hat and read them in the order they're drawn out,' Katie said. 'Now, what craft is everyone into? Knitting? Sewing? Macrame? Patchwork? Crochet? Découpage?'

By nine o'clock, coffee had been drunk, tentative friendships formed and a book-list drawn up – Judy Astley would start them off next week. Much to Katie's secret relief, *Jump* had been drawn fourth behind *Wolf Hall*, after which they would all surely be in need of a little light relief.

'Fingers crossed, I think the club is going to work,' Katie said as she locked the door and she and Mattie prepared to walk home. 'Everyone seems keen. And isn't Trisha talented? That patchwork quilt of hers is going to be absolutely beautiful.'

'Evening, Katie, ma'am. May I introduce you both to my dad, Noah Emprey Snr?'

Katie and Mattie turned to see Noah Jnr and his father smiling at them.

'Hi. Pleased to meet you, Mr Emprey. This is my godmother, Mattie.'

'Can we get you ladies a drink?' Noah Snr asked, looking across at the Dartmouth Arms.

Katie ignored the shake of Mattie's head. 'Thanks. Two white wines would be lovely.'

'Now why did you go and do that?' Mattie demanded as they watched the two men disappear into the pub to fetch the drinks. 'I don't want to drink with them.'

'Why are you being so rude?' Katie asked. 'It's not like you at all. They are very polite and friendly.'

'They're American.' Mattie shrugged at Katie's look of disbelief.

When the two Noahs reappeared with the drinks, they all moved to the small quay where Noah Jnr regarded the historical plaque fixed to the wall.

'The history in this place just blows my mind away. I can't get over the fact that one of my ancestors stood on this very quay.'

Mattie gave him a sharp look. 'Went over with the *Mayflower*, did they?'

'Yes, ma'am. My paternal family sailed with the Pilgrim Fathers,' Noah Snr answered. He took a sip of his beer. 'Like many Americans, I love knowing my roots are in the old country. Victoria, my daughter, who's arriving this weekend, is keen to trace our maternal English roots whilst we're over here.' He shrugged. 'But where to start? All we currently know is my great-great-grandmother was born somewhere in the West Country.' He looked at Mattie. 'You are so lucky to know exactly where you come from and where you stand in the order of things.'

'You Americans place far too much importance on past events,' Mattie said dismissively.

'You don't like Americans, ma'am?' Noah Snr asked.

'You're all right in small doses,' Mattie said.

'Surely the soldiers who were around for Operation Overlord were....'

'It was wartime and I was just a child,' Mattie interrupted. 'I didn't get to meet many. Besides, it's not something I want to discuss.'

'But what about Clara?' Katie said, not believing how uncharacteristically rude Mattie was being. 'She....'

'Katie, I've told you – the past is the past. Leave it alone. My childhood and my sister Clara are not up for discussion. End of. Now please can we go home? I have things to do. Goodnight, gentlemen.'

Turning on her heel, Mattie began to walk away.

Katie gave the Empreys an apologetic smile, muttered 'sorry,' and went after her.

They were back at the cottage before Mattie said, 'I'm sorry, Katie, but I find it impossible to talk about Clara with you, let alone with strangers, so can we please declare all talk of the war and Clara off limits?'

'If that's what you want,' Katie said quietly. 'But I still think you need to talk about things. Maybe even have some therapy sessions.'

'Pshaw!' Mattie said. 'Modern claptrap. Never felt the need to talk about things. Not about to start now. Right, think I'll have an early night. See you in the morning.'

Once in her room, Mattie sat on the edge of her bed. Was she turning into a grumpy old woman? Or was it just the effect any mention of the war and the Americans had on her? Clara had been such a taboo subject for so long, forced to stay in the deep recesses of her mind, that now people wanted to talk about her and the war years, it was impossible. Why were people so interested in hearing about a person they'd never met anyway?

She sighed. Now she wasn't working in the shop six days a week there was too much time to think about what might have been. About the life Clara's tragic death had in turn denied her.

Taken out of school at fifteen and made to work in A Good Yarn she'd yearned to escape – run away and see the world. Particularly America. Finding and meeting Hal's family had figured in her teenage dreams for a long time.

By the time she was twenty, though, her secret dreams had died as surely as Clara had. Resigned to a small-town life, she'd done the only thing left to her and accepted her lot.

But things had changed now that the shop was no longer her sole responsibility. Ironically, by giving Katie a way out from redundancy she'd made herself redundant. By taking over A Good Yarn, Katie had given her freedom for the first time in her life.

Freedom to do what, though? Charity work? More gardening? Take Bert for longer walks? Go away on the holiday she'd told Katie she intended to do? Well, it would be a start – and get her away from the Americans for a bit.

Mattie crossed over to the dressing table where she'd left the brochures the travel agent had given her. Tonight she'd choose a cruise and tomorrow she'd go into town and book a holiday. An urgent need to get away had rooted itself in her brain.

Six

Katie stepped back and regarded her handiwork. All four walls of the small room between the bathroom and the kitchen on the first floor, painted in two evenings. The cream paint with a hint of pale pink was already giving the unfurnished room a warm feeling. It was going to make a snug bedroom – all it needed now was a bed and possibly a wardrobe or chest of drawers. There wasn't room for both. And the boxes, moved from the clubroom where she and Leo had initially put them, stacked in the middle of the room, needed unpacking.

The list of things needed before she could move in was getting longer: a bed and a fridge were the most urgent. Thankfully the ancient electric cooker in the galley kitchen still worked and would do until something better turned up. She'd start looking in the local paper, see what was for sale, maybe try eBay. Hopefully there would be a few bargains around.

Pushing the lid tightly onto the paint tin, Katie took it out to the kitchen and put it with the rest of the decorating paraphernalia. The first floor was finished. Now she could concentrate on the attic room. Too late to start this evening but she'd have a look and work out what she was going to do – starting tomorrow.

Surprisingly it didn't need a lot doing to it. A good clean, definitely. Maybe paint the woodwork and it would be ready to furnish with her personal things.

Sitting in the ancient wicker chair by the window, Katie visualized the room as she wanted it: bookshelves and pictures, two cream sofas facing each other with a scarlet rug between them. There was a coffee table with a glass top in the kitchen. She'd bring that up to stand between the two settees. The chair she was sitting in could stay where it was by the skylight window.

The CD and DVD collection could go in the corner by the door and the TV would need a shelf or a small table to stand on. She'd need some curtains for the main windows that overlooked the river – not for privacy but to give the room a cosy feeling.

Katie sighed happily. Much as she loved living at Mattie's, it would be good to have her own space again. Mattie, too, must be finding it difficult to have someone in the cottage, having lived there on her own for so many years.

She glanced at her watch. Time for a quick phone call to Lara before she returned to Mattie's.

'Hi,' she said, when Lara answered. 'I'm at the flat. It's almost ready to move into. Another week at the most. I'm thinking of having a flat-warming party. You and Dexter down for the weekend again soon?'

'Could be if there's a party on offer,' Lara said. 'How's business?'

'Early days but ticking over. I've got nine members for the club now.'

'How's Patrick?'

'Haven't heard,' Katie said briefly. No point in giving Lara any ammunition to have a go at Patrick.

'Good.'

After a couple more minutes of general chat, Katie said, 'OK, time to leave you in peace. Give Daisy a cuddle for me. Ciao.'

Pushing the end-call button on her phone, Katie deliberated about phoning Patrick before throwing her phone back in her bag and going downstairs and locking up. Time to go home to Mattie. She wasn't going to chase after Patrick. If he was determined to ignore her and break off their relationship that way, so be it. It had been fun while it lasted.

Katie was unwrapping a delivery of some lace-weight yarn a few days later when Trisha arrived.

'Hi. Come to use the clubroom?'

'No. This is a gorgeous blue,' she said, fingering one of the balls, before adding: 'I wanted to ask – do you need a Saturday girl and can I be her if you do?'

'I do need someone – and for more than just Saturdays. But don't you want to hang out with your friends on Saturdays? Go up the line to Torquay for some fun? I know I used to jump on the train at every opportunity.'

Trisha shrugged. 'I'm there most days for college. I need to earn some money – my grant's all gone.'

'What are you studying at college?'

'Textiles and design. That's why it would be so perfect for

me to work here. Much better than waitressing. I can do more days in the holidays if you want, too. Please say yes.' Trisha bit a fingernail nervously as she looked at Katie.

'Can you stay now for a couple of hours? Trial run to see how you get on?'

'Great. I'll finish unpacking this lot, shall I?'

Katie soon realised Trisha was going to be a great asset. She quickly got the hang of working the till and remembered where things were when customers asked. By lunchtime, Katie felt confident enough to leave her for half an hour while she and Mattie walked Bert and picked up some sandwiches.

When they got back to A Good Yarn, Trisha was serving a customer and Noah Jnr was idly flicking through some postcards.

'I'm off,' Mattie muttered. 'See you at home later.'

'Hi, Katie,' Noah said. 'I've come to run Dad's latest idea past you.'

'He only wants us to dress up in 1940s clothes and be part of a re-enactment scene in his film,' Trisha said.

'Dad's idea is to show people going about their ordinary lives as the momentous events around them took place – a couple of authentic-looking scenes to open and close the film and a few more to use as a sort of link between things. We need to convey the atmosphere of the era.'

'My mum still talks about being an extra in *The Onedin Line* years ago,' Trisha said. 'Now it's my turn.'

Noah laughed. 'Whoa there, Trisha. We're not a big-budget TV series. We're very low key. Are you interested?' He turned to Katie. 'A Good Yarn was in business then, wasn't it?'

'Yes, but what it was selling apart from blackout material I have no idea,' Katie said. 'Would you want to film inside? Apart from the dresser behind the counter, it's changed. You should have been here a few weeks ago before Leo and I did some alterations.'

Noah shook his head. 'Just the door and the window, with you and Trisha standing in the doorway wearing clothes that convey the wartime era. We'd hope to film one evening after you close.'

'OK – provided Mattie agrees. She may not want you to feature the shop at all – in which case Noah Snr will have to look elsewhere for his evocative shot.'

When Katie got home later that evening, she found Mattie in a state of suppressed excitement.

'I've booked my cruise.'

'Great. Where and when?'

'It's called "Discovering the Riviera". Just look at the ship,' Mattie said, handing her a brochure full of coloured photographs.

'Wow. Impressive. When do you go?' Katie flicked through the brochure pages.

'Ah, that's the thing. I've taken a cancellation – the travel agent said I'd be silly to turn down such a good deal. I get a first-class cabin and all the extras for a silly price.'

Katie looked at her. 'When?' There was a pause before Mattie finally answered.

'Next Sunday.' She looked at Katie. 'You're sure you're OK with me going away so soon?'

'I think it's great. Wish I was coming with you.'

'But it's so soon,' Mattie said. 'I thought I'd be here to help you through the first couple of months and then go away.'

'I'll be fine,' Katie said. 'Now go and start packing. First write out a shopping list – you'll need some new clothes.'

Katie's mobile trilled as Mattie went upstairs. She automatically glanced at the caller ID before pressing the button. Patrick.

'Thought you'd forgotten all about me,' she said.

'Sorry. I've been busy. Look, there's a job I've heard about that if you're interested in, I can probably swing for you.'

'What sort of job and where?' Katie tried to sound polite and interested as she fiddled with the brochure Mattie had left on the table, but really what was Patrick thinking of? He knew she was committed down here now. From what he was saying, it sounded suspiciously like he was calling in a favour from someone.

'Assistant production manager up here in Bristol. Starting next week.'

Katie smothered a sigh. 'Patrick, there is no way I can come back up. The shop is open now and I have to give it my all. The job offer is too late for me.'

'You could at least say you'd think about it.'

'There is no way I can even think about taking a job like that at the moment.'

Silence.

'You haven't asked me how things are going down here.'

Another silence. Katie heard Patrick sigh before he spoke.

'So, how are things going? I still can't believe that you've thrown everything away by burying yourself down there.'

'I don't feel buried down here,' Katie said. 'Actually I'm enjoying it. I'll be moving into the flat over the shop soon. Come for a visit and see for yourself.'

'Too much going on up here to get away.'

'Even for a day?'

'Afraid so. I'll give you a ring in the week. Bye.'

'Bye,' Katie replied, but the line was already dead.

SEVEN

Mattie was quiet as Katie drove her to Totnes station early Sunday morning to catch the train to London, from where she'd fly to Nice before boarding the cruise ship. Deep in her own thoughts she didn't hear Katie's question the first time.

'Sorry, I was miles away. What did you say?'

'Whether you're happy about the filming at A Good Yarn going ahead?'

'Filming? Oh, I'd completely forgotten about it. I guess, if you and Trisha want to do it. Any publicity and all that,' Mattie said, before lapsing into silence again.

'Are you OK? You don't seem very happy for someone about to jet off to the South of France and the holiday of a lifetime.' Katie glanced at her, concerned.

Mattie sighed. 'I am looking forward to it,' she said. 'But I feel guilty abandoning you so soon. I should have gone on holiday later in the season. When you're more settled.'

'We both know the cancellation the agent offered you was too good to pass up. Besides you'll only be gone for ten days,' Katie said, concentrating on taking the right turning for the station's cafe parking area. 'We're not that busy in the shop yet. Trisha and I will be fine.'

'And lumbering you with Bert as well,' Mattie continued, shaking her head. 'I've told Leo that you'll ring him if there's an emergency or anything and he's promised to look in on you every day.'

'Mattie, you didn't! I'm a big girl now. I don't need Leo or anyone to keep an eye on me,' Katie said.

'Makes me feel better. Leo doesn't mind.'

Katie bit back the words 'No, but I do'. No point in upsetting Mattie before her holiday. She'd tell Leo herself to back off at the first sign of him interfering.

As the two of them walked across the footbridge linking the two platforms, Mattie said, 'I could cancel – say I'm ill. I'd get my money back then.' Mattie added thoughtfully, 'I did feel sick this morning.'

'Mattie, stop it. That was just excitement. You're going. You're going to have a fabulous time. Just make sure you look out for those shipboard Lotharios. Look, the train's coming,' Katie said. 'Promise me one thing, though?'

'What?'

'If there are any Americans on board – please don't push them overboard.'

Mattie laughed. 'Difficult, but OK, I promise.'

'Right, in you get,' and Katie carried Mattie's suitcase onto the train before quickly stepping back down onto the platform. 'Have a lovely time.'

By the time Mattie had struggled through several carriages and found her reserved seat, the train was hurtling through the Devonshire countryside. Smiling her thanks at the woman who stood up to let her reach her window seat, Mattie sat down.

Staring out at the passing scenery, Mattie tried to quell her misgivings. Hopefully Katie was right and she would have a fabulous cruise but she still wasn't convinced she'd made the right decision going away so soon after Katie had taken over the shop. At least Leo would be keeping an eye on her, whether Katie appreciated it or not.

It was strange being alone in Mattie's home that evening and Katie moved around restlessly. Bert too was missing his mistress, nuzzling into Katie's hand every now and again for reassuring strokes.

'Sorry, old boy, afraid you've got to make do with me for a bit,' Katie said, giving him an extra biscuit and a cuddle.

Standing by the kitchen window, she looked out across the river towards Kingswear where street- and house-lights were beginning to twinkle in the evening dusk.

What would she have been doing this weekend if she'd still been in Bristol? No doubt Patrick would have persuaded her to go to an art gallery Saturday afternoon and the evening would have been spent watching some foreign film with incomprehensible subtitles before going on to a late night party in the trendy Waterside area where Patrick lived. Sunday would have meant the Sunday papers in bed, a late lunch with friends before returning to her own flat and getting ready for another week at work.

Patrick had no doubt continued his weekends in the same vein. Maybe he'd already found someone to replace the part she'd played in his life.

What would her life have been like now if she'd never left down here, if she'd settled for a job on the local paper, married a local boy, perhaps become a farmer's wife – had a child – children? Mentally, Katie shook herself.

Pointless going down the road of hypothetical questions. Like Mattie kept insisting: the past was the past. The present was all that mattered and the future of A Good Yarn. Making herself a coffee, Katie decided to try to work on the shop accounts.

Half an hour later she sighed, closed the laptop and pushed it away. It was no use, she couldn't concentrate any more.

Her mobile phone rang, shattering the quiet and making her jump. Noah Snr.

'Katie, it's Noah Snr here. I was wondering if we can film you and Trisha tomorrow evening?' he asked. 'About 6.30? I'll get Noah Jnr to drop some clothes in for you to choose something from during the day.'

'Fine. Any idea how long it will take?'

'An hour at the most. And then I've reserved a table at the hotel for dinner as a thank-you. I hope you and Trisha are free?'

'I am,' Katie said. 'I'll check with Trisha. Thank you.' As she ended the call, Bert began barking frantically at the front door.

'Katie, open the door. It's me. Leo.'

'What are you doing here?'

'Thought you might appreciate some company? I've brought supper.'

'Look, I know you've promised Mattie you'll keep an eye on me while she's away, but this is a bit over the top, isn't it?' Katie said as Leo proceeded to empty a carrier bag of food onto the table.

Leo shook his head. 'No, we've both got to eat, might as well do it together. It's not a gourmet meal. Just cold roast chicken and salad, followed by raspberries and clotted cream – still your favourite?'

Katie smiled and gave in to the inevitable. 'Definitely. OK. Mattie left some wine in the fridge – I'll fetch the glasses.'

'This is delicious,' she said minutes later. 'I hadn't realized I was so hungry.'

'Mattie get away all right this morning?' Leo asked.

'Yes, although she was threatening to cancel almost up to the moment she got on the train,' Katie said. 'I think she was worried about being on her own.'

'She'll soon make friends once she's on board the boat,' Leo said, helping himself to more chicken.

'Do you know what it is with Mattie and her dislike of all things American? Is your Dad the same? And Clara? Does he ever mention her? Mattie absolutely refuses to discuss anything to do with Clara – her own sister!'

'No, Dad's not bothered about Americans. As for Aunt Clara, well she's pretty much a forgotten subject in our house but I know she dreamed of being a GI bride, which my grandparents forbade when Operation Tiger happened and changed everything anyway.'

Katie took a sip of wine. 'It's strange, isn't it, how when you're growing up, the adults around you are just that, adults. The fact that my parents, your parents, Mattie, all had a life with their own desires, ambitions and secrets never entered my head for a single moment.'

'It's a generation thing,' Leo said. 'The new generation

regards the old one as just that, old and of no interest. Until they start to get older too and finally realize that no one is unique.'

'Do you know how Clara died?'

'No.'

Katie put her glass down and fiddled with the pepper grinder in the centre of the table. 'The thing is, I think Mattie could do with talking to someone about Clara. These days she'd be offered counselling to help with a tragedy like losing a sister, but I bet all that time ago it was a question of keeping a stiff upper lip. Clara's death had a huge effect on Mattie's life.'

'If Mattie doesn't want to talk about it, even now, there's not a lot you can do,' Leo said.

'Leo?' Katie hesitated and Leo looked at her, waiting.

'Do you think I've done the right thing coming back? Taking on the shop? Maybe it would have been better for Mattie to have sold up and made a complete break of things. She'd have enough money in the bank to give her a good life.'

'I think you've done exactly the right thing for Mattie,' Leo said. 'Whether you've done the right thing for you, is the question.' He looked at her thoughtfully.

'Actually I'm really enjoying being back down here. My main worry is Mattie – and hoping I can make the shop a success like she's convinced I will.' Katie sighed. 'There's so much that can go wrong: a rainy summer with no tourists, the locals not supporting the club, stocking the wrong things….'

'Tiggy, stop it. You always did over-analyze things. Mattie

will come back from her holiday reinvigorated and you're going to make A Good Yarn into a runaway success.'

He poured the last of the wine into their glasses. 'How's the flat shaping up? I've got some free time so I could come and give you a hand with things.'

'I've sorted the first floor. Need to organize some furniture – like a bed and a table and chairs. I'm starting on the attic room next. Luckily it doesn't need much doing to it.'

'There's an auction out Cornworthy way soon. The Old Vicarage is being sold. I could run you out there – take a trailer with us, in case you buy anything.'

'Sounds great, thanks. As for helping with the attic room, you've done so much already, I can't expect you to do any more.'

Leo opened his mouth to protest but sighed instead, before downing his wine in one go.

EIGHT

Trisha turned up at the shop late Monday afternoon to try to find something she was happy to wear for the filming.

'These are gruesome, aren't they?' she said, inspecting the bag Noah Jnr had left earlier. 'I was hoping to wear something pretty. And where's the make-up girl?'

Katie laughed. 'Oh, Trisha, I don't think there will be a make-up girl. Women didn't wear much in those days and I think Noah Snr wants us to look as ordinary as possible.'

'No chance of looking anything but ordinary in these things,' Trisha grumbled.

'Think there was a dearth of attractive things around during the war,' Katie said. 'Clothing coupons were rationed and it was a case of mend and make-do for most people. What about these?' she added, as she pulled out a woollen navy pleated skirt with a matching jacket. 'Look, here's a beret and a pair of shoes.'

Trisha pulled a face before disappearing into the back room to try the things on. Katie found herself a brown trench coat with a belt that would go over her own clothes and a pair of thick knitted stockings to go with some brown lace-up brogues. As she tied a patterned scarf over her head Noah

Jnr arrived with a young woman clutching a clipboard and a wicker basket. Bert gave them both an enthusiastic welcome.

'Oh, what a shame you're not an old-fashioned Labrador,' the young woman said, bending down to pet him. 'You could have been in the film then.'

'Katie, meet my sister Vicky. Dad's put her in charge of continuity – making her do some work for a change.' Noah laughed as his sister poked her tongue out at him.

'Hi, Katie, good to meet you,' Vicky said. 'Can you put some wool and wooden needles in this, please?' she added, as she handed Katie a wicker basket. 'Some navy wool would be ideal – otherwise something dark. I need you to carry it for the scene. Thanks.'

Just then, Trisha appeared in her costume. 'This is gross. I wish I hadn't told my boyfriend to come and watch, now.'

'You'll need to take off that gold bracelet and your earrings, please,' Vicky said, looking at Trisha. 'They're too modern. Otherwise you're fine.'

'Right,' Noah said. 'Let's get started.'

A small crowd had gathered in the street to watch the filming and Trisha self-consciously waved to a long-haired boy standing next to Ron, the Blackawton cousin. 'He's only gone and brought his granddad too,' she moaned.

Katie stood still and looked at her. Trisha was dating Ron's grandson? Now why did that knowledge fill her with apprehension?

The two Noahs and Vicky were waiting for her in the lounge of the Castle Hotel when Katie arrived alone later that evening.

'Sorry. Am I very late? Bert wouldn't settle when I took him home. He's missing Mattie,' she explained breathlessly.

'No problem,' Noah Snr said. 'Where's Trisha?'

'Sends her apologies but she's had to go somewhere urgent with her boyfriend, Gary, and his granddad,' Katie said. 'She's promised to join us later.' She kept her misgivings over what exactly Trisha was doing with Ron Blackawton to herself.

'Noah Jnr is so cute,' she'd said excitedly, when Katie had told her about the dinner invitation. 'His accent is cool. I'd love a proper date with him.'

So what or who had made Trisha change her mind about having dinner at the hotel with the Empreys? Her boyfriend? Or his grandfather? Just how close was Trisha to the Blackawton cousins? Tomorrow at work she'd have a chat with her. Warn her not to discuss wool shop business with Gary or Ron.

'Shall we go up to the restaurant?' Noah Snr said. 'They've promised us a table overlooking the Boat Float and river.'

'I haven't been in here for years,' Katie said as they began to make their way through the hotel to the Grill Room. 'My mum used to bring me sometimes after ballet on a Saturday morning as a special treat. Felt really grown-up sipping my orange juice in the Galleon Bar – especially if any of the naval cadets from the college were in.'

'We've seen some old photos taken during the time Operation Overlord was swinging into action and the interior was totally different then. Full of American soldiers too,' Noah said. 'Wish we could turn the clock back for a day.

Filming modern history in an ancient town has its problems, that's for sure.' He shrugged his shoulders as Katie looked at him.

'It's difficult to convey mid-twentieth-century events taking place in all these medieval buildings and streets, which is why the re-enactments in the appropriate clothes are so important. At least the coastline and the beaches have stayed relatively the same through the years.'

'How's filming going generally? People willing to talk a bit more?' Katie asked.

Vicky laughed. 'Dad's tearing his hair out. He can usually charm information out of anybody but you people are so private.'

'Details regarding Operation Overlord aren't too difficult to dig up,' Noah Jnr said. 'But nobody really wants to talk about that time at all. As for Operation Tiger,' he shrugged, 'everyone is in mass denial and the rumours abound. If it wasn't for that tank in Slapton you could be forgiven for thinking it had never happened.'

Noah Snr raised his glass in a toast to Katie. 'Thank you for your help anyway. Now tell us how you've ended up running a wool shop.'

Katie placed her hand over her glass as the waiter went to pour more wine. 'No more, thanks. It was Mattie's suggestion when I was made redundant. The big surprise is how much I'm actually enjoying it – and living back down here again.'

'Home towns always have a special place in one's heart,' Noah Snr said.

'Mattie would say that was typical American sentimentality if she were here,' Katie laughed. 'But I think you're right.'

'Mattie had a hard time growing up here during the war?' Vicky asked.

'I don't think it was any harder for her than most of her generation,' Katie said quietly. 'The death of her sister after the war seems to have affected her more than anything. I think the problem is she wasn't ever encouraged to talk about it and she bottled up all her emotions. It's probably too late now but I think she needs to talk it all out with someone.'

'Maybe it would pave the way if we could persuade her to talk to us about things she remembers,' Noah said.

'You could try but I don't hold out much hope,' Katie said. 'Very stubborn is Mattie. I'm hoping her Mediterranean cruise will help her relax.'

Vicky laughed. 'Our great-grandmother was like that. So's Grandma Elizabeth. You can't make her do a thing she doesn't want to, can you, Dad?'

'No. Currently I'm trying to persuade her to come to Europe for a holiday before we finish filming,' Noah Snr said to Katie. 'Won't even consider the idea. Says she's too busy dealing with my late grandmother's effects after she died three months ago.'

'Must be a difficult time for her,' Katie said. 'Especially if she and her mother were close?'

Noah nodded. 'They were.'

'I'll try to uncover some more family history over here,' Vicky said. 'That might work. She's fascinated by genealogy,' she added in an aside to Katie.

Katie was trying to choose between a delicious-sounding crème brûlée and a dish of nougat parfait with raspberry compote when a breathless Trisha arrived.

'Oh good. You're still here. Sorry I'm so late. Am I too late to eat? Only I'm starving.'

'I'm sure they'll find you something,' Noah Snr said, catching the attention of a waitress.

'So what was so important that Gary wanted?' Katie couldn't help asking.

Trisha shrugged. 'Just something his granddad insisted had to be done tonight.' Smiling, she accepted a glass of wine Noah Jnr poured her and turned back to Katie.

'Have to tell you before I forget – I can't work tomorrow morning. Sorry.'

About to protest it was short notice and she was letting her down, Katie bit her tongue. The restaurant wasn't the place to argue with Trisha over work, so she simply said, 'OK. Tomorrow afternoon?'

'Afternoon is fine,' Trisha said.

'Good. I want to talk to you then too.'

It was almost eleven o'clock when Katie said her goodbyes to everyone, declining an offer of an escort home from Noah Snr. 'I'll be fine. It's not far and there are still people about.'

As she reached the steps in Fairfax Place she jumped as Leo fell into step beside her.

'Switched your phone off?'

'No. It's in my bag as usual,' Katie said, not adding that she could never hear it ringing in there. 'Why?'

'I've been ringing and texting you for over an hour, that's why.'

'What's wrong? It's not Mattie, is it?'

'Somebody broke into the shop tonight,' Leo said. 'Hey, where are you going?'

'Stupid question. The shop of course,' Katie said, turning away and beginning to run towards Lower Street.

'Nothing you can do tonight,' Leo protested. 'I've made sure everything is secure now.'

'How?' Katie flung the question over her shoulder as she continued running.

'Mattie left me her spare keys.'

She might have guessed Mattie would leave her keys with Leo. All contingencies covered. 'Is there much damage? How did they get in?'

'Through the clubroom window. No real damage as far as I could see but they have messed things up a bit.'

Katie was panting when they reached the shop and took several deep breaths while Leo unlocked the door. 'Be careful where you tread,' he warned.

Katie had difficulty in holding back the tears when she saw the state of the shop. Leo's 'They've messed things up a bit' had failed to prepare her for what greeted her as she pushed open the door. There was wool all over the floor, several shelves had been swept clean – their contents strewn all over. The postcard stand had been tipped upside down, kits and jewellery were flung together in a heap. Total mayhem.

'Why do people do things like this?' she said.

'Any number of reasons. Way things are these days,' Leo said. 'You'll have to check if there's anything missing in the morning. Right now I think you should go home.'

'You sure everything is secure?'

'Katie, I told you I've sorted it. Nothing you can do until the morning. Come on, I'll walk you home. And do me a favour in future, will you? Keep your phone where you can hear it.'

NINE

Mattie waited until the white-gloved butler had closed the door behind him before sinking down onto a chair. From the moment she'd been handed a flute of champagne as she embarked, reality had been ebbing away from her. Now, looking around what was to be her home for the next ten days she was speechless.

Her first-class cabin had turned out to be a suite and was as luxurious as Mattie had been promised. She'd never been so close to such luxury before. The marble and gold in the bathroom would have done justice to a palace. As for the queen-size bed with its creamy cotton sheets, featherweight duvet and the pillows she'd chosen from the selection the butler had offered her – she almost wished it was bedtime so she could sink down into a blissful sleep.

The spacious saloon reminded Mattie of a drawing room she'd once seen in a *Homes and Gardens* magazine. Thick cream carpet, a sofa and three chairs covered in a Mediterranean blue material, table lamps standing on polished occasional tables and a small bureau in one corner with personalized stationery. It was, the butler had assured her, 'large enough for you to entertain the friends you will make on board'.

She went across to the bathroom and opened the door. Bigger than her bathroom at home, there was a vast array of all the soaps and toiletries she could ever want lined up on the sink vanity unit. Large soft towels were on the towel rail; a white bathrobe hung on the hook. As soon as she'd unpacked she'd take a shower.

There was no sign of her suitcases in the bedroom. They'd been whisked away at embarkation as the champagne had been placed in her hand and she'd assumed they would be placed ready for her in the cabin. So where were they? Uncertain as to what she should do, Mattie wished she'd asked the butler where they were before he'd left.

The modern unit in the bedroom had several drawers and a wardrobe to one side. Absently Mattie opened the door, wondering about hangers – she hadn't packed any – to find all her clothes hanging up neatly on padded hangers, her shoes lined up on the rack at the bottom. Pulling open one of the dressing unit drawers she saw her underwear neatly folded. Thank God Katie had insisted she went shopping for new clothes before her holiday. Imagine the embarrassment if the butler, or whoever had done her unpacking, had seen her old underwear. In another drawer were her blouses and cardigans.

The butler had left the glass doors leading to her private veranda open and hearing the ship's hooter give a warning sound, Mattie wandered out. They were casting off and manoeuvring their way out to the open sea. She sat for some time in the cushion-loaded Lloyd Loom chair, watching the Nice shoreline fade into the distance, before turning back into her suite. A shower and then she would go exploring before dinner.

Carefully closing her cabin door behind her, Mattie made her way along the carpeted corridor towards the main part of the ship. The glossy brochure she'd looked at back in her cottage had in no way prepared her for what she found.

She was on board a floating palace. There was no other way to describe it. Thick carpet in all the main areas, chandeliers hanging in the shopping mall with its designer label outlets, the intimate theatre, the spa, the library, the restaurants, the pool. There was so much, so many opportunities for pleasure and for relaxing.

Clutching several activity sheets, which a helpful girl at the information desk near the entrance to the shopping mail had pressed on her, Mattie wandered out on deck. Bypassing the swimming pool with its attendant sun-loungers, Mattie found herself a deckchair at the far end of the top deck and settled down to decide how she would spend the rest of the day and plan her itinerary for tomorrow.

A steward appeared at her side. 'Madame would like a drink?'

About to decline with her customary politeness, she changed her mind. She was thirsty. 'A long, cold, non-alcoholic one would be nice,' she said and settled back to await its arrival.

Looking through all the various things on offer she could do, Mattie decided she'd spend the rest of the day quietly, have dinner in the Gourmet Restaurant and then spend the evening in her cabin with a book from the library. An early night in that comfortable bed beckoned after her day of travelling.

Tomorrow she would swim, book herself a massage in the spa, have her hair done, maybe even have a manicure. Somehow this glamorous ship made her feel she'd be letting it down if she didn't make an effort to look her best.

Sipping the elaborate pink drink with its umbrella and swizzle stick floating in some creamy froth the steward had returned with, Mattie looked around at her fellow passengers. She was the only woman on her own. Everyone else was part of a couple.

Mattie, used to being on her own, had thought she wouldn't mind holidaying as such but now, looking at the happy people around her, she wasn't so sure. It would have been fun to be able to turn to someone and say, 'This drink is amazing,' or 'That woman's dress is a lovely colour,' but there was no-one she could share such thoughts with.

Still, it was only the first day of her holiday, she was sure to meet some of her fellow passengers tonight in the restaurant. There had to be other single people on board. And tomorrow night the butler had told her she was to dine at the captain's table. She was looking forward to that.

Twenty-four hours later and Mattie was surprised at how much she was enjoying life on board. She'd enjoyed her day, had met some lovely people who'd invited her to join them for lunch and now she was taking her new red cocktail dress with its sequins out of the wardrobe and preparing to meet the captain.

She looked at herself in the full-length mirror and barely recognized the woman reflected. The dress Katie had helped her choose, insisting that she would need something glamorous to wear for evenings on board, fitted her perfectly. The hairdresser that morning had not only talked her into having her hair restyled but had insisted some lowlights would also be a good idea. The strappy shoes on her feet had heels which, whilst not in the Christian Lacroix league, were certainly higher than the comfy court shoes she normally wore. Picking up her evening bag from the table, Mattie hoped she could live up to this new persona of hers that somehow she'd managed to create today.

Throwing a pashmina over her shoulders, Mattie left the suite and made her way to the dining room. As she hovered uncertainly by the entrance, a tall man already in the room walked across to her and escorted her to the table.

'I am Henri,' he said, formally shaking her hand. 'We are both alone, I think, so we sit together for dinner?'

'Mattie,' she said, noting his French accent and grateful for his suggestion. Being on her own for dinner, surrounded by couples, had been a daunting prospect. 'Thank you.'

'You enjoy the cruise so far?' Henri asked.

Mattie smiled. 'The ship is unbelievable. I've never seen anything like it before. There's so much to do – as for the food ...'

'It is always the same – so much temptation. It is your first time on a cruise?'

'Actually it's my first time away from England too,' she said. What on earth had prompted her to tell such a suave man that? She must sound like a pathetic old woman.

Henri simply smiled. 'You have chosen well. We visit some lovely places this week but one you must not miss is the Ile St Honorat when we anchor off Cannes. It is one of my most favourite places in the world.'

'You know it well?'

'*Oui*. I was born in Cannes. Now I live in Paris. My wife was Parisian,' Henri said. 'No matter how hard I tried I couldn't get her to leave. Not even for the Côte d'Azur.' He gestured towards the distant coastline. 'But now,' he shrugged, 'I think I may finally return.'

'Your wife has died?' Mattie asked gently.

'A year ago. I am slowly adjusting to life without her.'

Mattie touched him on the arm. 'I am so sorry.'

Leaving the captain's table later that evening, they went to the ship's ornate theatre together and watched the variety show before Henri insisted on them sharing a nightcap in the Cocktail Bar.

Henri told her about his life in Paris. In return Mattie told him about Katie taking over A Good Yarn and a little of her life – that to her ears sounded so ordinary compared to his. But Henri was an attentive and interested listener.

'And family? You have some?'

'A brother and two nephews. I would have loved children, but I never married so it never happened.' Mattie stared reflectively out at the Mediterranean sea as it glistened in the moonlight. 'But Katie is like a daughter to me.'

'You are lucky in that at least,' Henri said. 'Cecile never wanted children, so we never had any. It is something I regret but,' he shrugged his shoulders, 'c'est la vie.'

Henri insisted on escorting her to her cabin and gave her a gentle goodnight kiss on the cheek as he left her.

'Katie warned me about shipboard Lotharios,' Mattie said, looking at him.

Henri laughed. 'I'm French. It is the custom. *Bonne nuit.*'

Once in her cabin, Mattie slipped off her shoes, opened the veranda door and sat for some time simply looking out at the moon shining over the Mediterranean and listening to the noise of the sea as the ship made its way. She sighed contentedly. A perfect end to a wonderful day. And this was just the beginning of her holiday.

TEN

After a restless night when sleep eluded her, Katie was up early. With Mattie away she'd got in the habit of walking Bert out to Gallants Bower before breakfast in the morning but the break-in at the shop last night changed things. She was desperate to get down to A Good Yarn, start the cleaning up and see what was actually missing.

'Sorry, Bert,' she said now, clipping his lead on. 'It's straight to the shop this morning. We'll have a longer walk later.'

The mess, if anything, looked worse in daylight and Bert, trying to get to his usual basket under the counter without treading on things, looked up at her as if to ask what was going on.

Stifling a sigh, Katie went through to the clubroom where everything was equally chaotic – furniture turned over, books on the floor, tea and coffee thrown everywhere. Standing there trying to fight back the tears she didn't protest when Leo arrived and took her in his arms.

'Hey, Tiggy, we'll get it sorted.'

'What if the club members had left their work here? It would have been ruined. Why?'

Leo shrugged. 'Maybe somebody wants to put you out of business before you start properly.'

'Blackawton cousins?'

'Could be. I'll do some asking around and see if I can uncover anything. What time is Trisha coming in?'

'Later. She told me last night she couldn't come in this morning.' Katie's voice trailed away. 'You don't think?'

'Nice kid but she's with Ron's grandson and if it turns out Ron is involved....' Leo let the sentence hang in the air.

'I'll have to sack her, won't I?' Katie moved out of the circle of Leo's arms.

'Maybe, but don't jump to conclusions just yet. Right, I suggest we start operation clean-up in the shop.'

As they went through to the shop, the door was pushed open and a policeman entered. 'Made a bit of a mess in here, haven't they? Anything missing?'

'Hard to tell at the moment,' Katie said, moving behind the counter. 'But the till is empty.'

'Much in it?'

'Just the daily float of twenty pounds,' Katie said. 'That's all I ever leave.'

'Gather they got in through an open window?' the policeman said. 'So no signs of a forced entry. My guess? It's kids looking for drug money, didn't find enough and trashed things just for the fun of it.'

'It's all right to start clearing up, isn't it?' Katie asked. 'I don't want to destroy any evidence but I do need to get the shop open.'

'You go ahead. Doubt it's worth waiting for the finger-print boys. They may call in to take a look at the window.

Drop a note of any items that you discover are missing into the station and we'll take it from there. But don't hold your breath,' he added, as he turned to leave. 'Too much of this kind of thing going on these days.'

Katie sighed. 'Better get to it, I suppose.' She looked at Leo. 'I can manage. You don't have to stay. I'm sure you've got lots of farm things to do.'

'Nothing that won't keep for a couple of hours.'

'Thanks. Best make a start on the shop. Leave the club-room till later, I think,' Katie said.

As they worked together sorting things out, Leo said, 'You need a burglar alarm.'

Katie placed a damaged tapestry kit on the pile of things she was hoping to salvage and sell on cut-price. 'Well at least the flat is nearly finished. As soon as Mattie gets back I'll move in. Living on the premises will be far more of a deterrent than a burglar alarm.'

'Katie Teague, if you believe that, you'll believe anything. You on your own here, coping with burglars, doesn't bear thinking about. No. I'll organize an alarm system for you and I insist you stay at Mattie's until it's up and running.'

'Leo Cranford, stop bossing me about. You know I've always planned to live upstairs. It'll be sooner rather than later now.'

The shop door pinged and Trisha appeared. 'Hi. I'm sorry about this morning. Had to go into college for a face to face with the head of the department. Hey, what's been going on here?'

'Break-in last night,' Leo said. 'Hadn't you heard?'

Trisha shook her head. 'No.'

'About last night, Trisha,' Katie said. 'Why were you so late joining us at the hotel for dinner?'

'I told you. Gary needed me to help him with something his granddad insisted could only be done last night. Actually I think he was jealous at the idea of me going out to dinner with the Empreys.'

'You were with Gary and his granddad?' Leo asked.

'Yes. Why? Oh, I get it. You think Ron turned this place over because he wants to get his hands on it – and you think I had something to do with it. Thanks a bunch.' Trisha turned and flounced out of the shop, banging the door behind her.

Katie sighed. 'That went well.'

From the very first day of her holiday Mattie embraced the laid-back atmosphere on board. Her whole purpose in life for the ten days of her holiday was to enjoy herself, and the crew on board – who were ready to pander to her every need – made sure she did.

The days seemed to go on forever, stretching into the distance like long-ago childhood days with no adult worries to hamper simple enjoyment. The cabin was always immaculate whenever she returned to it, the towels were changed every day and each evening the bed was turned down and a luxury chocolate placed on her pillow. A perfect end to the day.

Her days all started with a leisurely breakfast, sitting on her private veranda watching the sea and planning her day's activities with the aid of the daily bulletin she found in her cabin every evening. So many ideas. The days they were in port offered a selection of excursions but if she elected to stay on board, she could get fit, learn photography, inspect the kitchens and have a cookery lesson, play bridge or bingo and even learn to scuba dive. Or, she could choose to do nothing more energetic than take a book out of the well-stocked library and sit on deck, reading.

Today though, she planned a swim before attending a lecture in the theatre on 'Saving the World's Bees', and then a visit to the shopping mall was on her agenda. It had dawned on her last night that the few clothes she'd brought with her were not enough for all the on-board socializing that went on, so she planned to treat herself to at least two new outfits, maybe a dress, a top and possibly a pair of shoes. Secretly she'd also promised herself to try on the pair of cream palazzo trousers she'd seen in the boutique at the end of the mall – so different from her normal style but they did look elegant.

After her shopping she was meeting Henri and another couple for lunch in the Rendezvous Bar on the top deck. Ah, Henri. Thoughtfully she put the bulletin down on the table. He really was a dear and seemed to have taken it on himself to be her guide and companion for the holiday.

Mattie poured herself another glass of orange juice. She knew she looked a different woman to the one who'd stepped on board such a short time ago, but underneath she was still the same ordinary person she'd always been. If it hadn't been for the cancellation she would be in a cabin somewhere in the bowels of the ship, a long way from this luxurious deck where both she and Henri had suites.

On a ship as large as this one, she doubted that their paths would ever have crossed. They certainly wouldn't have met at the captain's table – an honour she knew was not extended to more modest passengers.

But they had met and she was pleased to have his company – so much of the socializing was new to her but with Henri at her side it was easier to cope with. Mattie knew he'd automatically travel first class wherever and however he went. He'd laughed when she'd told him about the cancellation and that he shouldn't think she normally had first-class suites – first-class anything really.

ELEVEN

Katie was at home giving Bert his evening meal when Leo rang.

'That auction I told you about is tomorrow afternoon. Can you get away for an hour or two?'

'Yes. It's one of Trisha's days for working.'

'Still working for you, then?'

'She came and apologized for flouncing out and begged to stay,' Katie said. 'I told her she could, but under no circumstances was she to talk about the shop to either Gary or his granddad. She's promised not to, so hopefully....' Katie sighed. 'The thing is, I really need her – especially while Mattie is away.'

'Pick you up at about 12 then,' Leo said.

'That early?'

'Viewing opens at 11.30. Auction starts at two o'clock. You'll need to have a look around first.'

'Not sure I can leave Trisha on her own for that long,' Katie said.

'Sure you can. She'll cope. I'll see you tomorrow.'

Easy enough for Leo to say Trisha would cope on her own for several hours, Katie thought, ending the call. But if she wanted to go to the auction there was no alternative, with Mattie away, and she did need to get some furniture organized for the flat, ready for her to move in next week.

'You've got my mobile number,' she said to Trisha the next morning. 'Any problems, ring and I'll come straight back.'

'There won't be any problems,' Trisha said.

'Can you remember to give everybody one of the Knit in Public leaflets, please?' Katie said, indicating the pile on the counter. 'Need to start drumming up interest.'

'Will do. Now go, Leo's outside. Have fun.'

Sitting next to Leo as they drove down narrow lanes in the countryside behind Dartmouth, Katie pushed worrying thoughts about leaving Trisha in charge for so long to the back of her mind.

'Is there a catalogue or anything for this sale?' she said.

Leo shook his head. 'No. It's all very low-key – doubt there will be any valuable antiques.'

As they joined the queue of cars waiting to park in a field next to the large country house where the auction was, Katie said, 'Might be low key but there certainly seems to be plenty of interest.'

'Lots of nosy parkers, I expect,' Leo said, looking around. Once they'd parked they followed a sequence of blue arrow 'Entrance' signs and found themselves by a pair of weather-beaten wrought-iron gates at the head of a rhododendron-flanked drive.

The Georgian house that came into view, as they rounded the last of the bends in the drive, had once been a beautiful house. Now run down, a sad looking air of desolation hung around it.

'Do you know what's happening to the house?' Katie asked. 'Has somebody local bought it?'

'Developers again,' Leo said briefly.

'Oh, that's a shame. It would be lovely to restore it properly,' Katie said. 'Can't wait to see the inside.'

'You go ahead,' Leo said. 'I want to look at the stuff in the barn. I'll find you in there.'

The old wooden front door, with its black studs and iron hinges, was open and Katie could see people milling around in the marble-tiled hallway where an imposing wooden staircase dominated the large open space.

Trestle tables with boxes of books and miscellaneous assorted things were scattered around with people rummaging through before moving on.

Once inside Katie wandered from drawing room to dining room to kitchen, marvelling at the size of the rooms. In its heyday the house must have been very grand indeed. Austere family portrait pictures still lined the walls either side of the staircase and the drawing room, with its four full-length windows overlooking a terrace, was full of religious oil paintings.

Katie was standing looking out over the terrace where lichened eagles with outspread wings were still defiantly guarding the worn and weed-strewn flight of stone steps leading down to an unkempt lawn, when Leo found her.

'Found anything you want yet?' he asked.

'Haven't started to look properly,' Katie confessed. 'I was daydreaming about what the house must have been like in its heyday.' She smiled. 'I've spent months in the past looking for authentic houses like this to use for film and TV costume dramas. Too much to hope, I suppose, that the developers keep it in period. They could earn a lot of money with it then.' She turned to Leo. 'Right. I must concentrate. That bookcase would fit in the alcove and that gate-leg table would be useful too,' she said, pointing towards the back of the room. 'I quite like this picture,' she said, crossing over to look at a watercolour. '*Sailing in the Dart*,' she said, reading the inscription on the frame. '1925.'

'Been upstairs yet?'

Katie shook her head.

'Come on, then,' Leo said.

Dutifully, Katie followed Leo up the wide staircase and into the first bedroom they came to. Katie laughed as she saw the huge four-poster bed that virtually filled the room. 'I'll pass on that, I think.'

By the time the auction started, Katie had earmarked several of the lots but despaired of being lost in the crowd surrounding the auctioneer.

'You'll have to bid for me,' she told Leo. 'At least he'll see you.'

Within an hour Leo had successfully bid on a bed, a pine chest of drawers, an easy chair, the coffee table, the book-case, the sailing picture, a box of miscellaneous bits, a square of carpet and a bundle of material that Katie had found in a corner. She'd lost out on a few things – including a fridge and a scarlet rug she'd imagined under her coffee table but on the whole she'd found more than she'd expected to.

'Right, you go and pay for this lot,' Leo said. 'I'll fetch the car and trailer.'

Leo was waiting for her by the time she'd paid for everything and together they started to collect and load the stuff into the trailer. Leo enlisted the help of a couple of porters for the bed and other furniture and the trailer was soon loaded.

'Are you ready for this lot in the flat?' Leo asked as they turned onto the Dartmouth road heading home. 'Space in the barn if not.'

'Can we take it to the flat, please,' Katie said. 'The bedroom is ready for the bed and the drawers. The attic room is almost finished so the other bits and pieces can go straight up there, even if we just put them in the middle of the floor.'

Trisha was waiting for them when they got back and gave a hand carrying stuff indoors.

'Busy afternoon?' Katie said, as they manhandled the bed-frame up the stairs.

'No more than usual,' Trisha said. 'Couple of the club members came in for an hour. Oh, I did sell the last of that blue Debbie Bliss wool.'

'Should be some more in this week,' Katie said. She watched Leo screw the bed base together and then push it into position against the wall.

'I'll order a mattress tonight off the internet. Once that arrives I can move in.' She smiled at Leo, daring him to give her one of his 'stay up at Mattie's' lectures.

TWELVE

The evening before the ship was due to moor in Cannes Bay, Henri mentioned the Ile St Honorat excursion again, as they strolled along the promenade deck after their now-routine nightcap together.

'We go together yes? It will be my pleasure to be your guide and show you the island.'

'Is it really worth a visit?' Mattie asked. 'I was thinking I'd skip it and do the shopping trip in Cannes itself instead.'

Henri shook his finger at her. '*Non*. Shopping you can do in Monaco when we get there. You and I will both refresh our souls on St Honorat, ready to face the real world again next week.'

'OK you win,' Mattie said, wondering why Henri thought she was in need of refreshing her soul. Was it something she'd said or did she look tired and world-weary?

The first thing that struck Mattie the next day as she and Henri stepped ashore from the motor launch that ferried them and a few of their fellow passengers from the cruise ship, was the sheer tranquillity on the island. Even the air smelt different. It was hard to believe that across the bay the frantic life of the French Riviera was in full swing.

'If we're quick we may just catch the end of the morning service,' Henri said, indicating a pair of high wrought-iron gates at the head of a path leading towards the abbey.

Obediently Mattie followed Henri along the path with its columns and formal flower bed, where signs sternly ordered 'Silence' from everyone. Entering the dimly lit chapel and standing at the back, Mattie listened as the monks effortlessly performed their morning ritual chants before slowly leaving, the long skirts of their white Cistercian order flapping around their legs.

Mattie and Henri stayed still for several moments, both lost in their own thoughts and savouring the centuries-old special atmosphere that surrounded them.

'That was so beautiful,' Mattie whispered as they finally turned to leave. 'Thank you. You were right. That was something not to be missed. Hearing the monks sing will stay with me forever.'

Making their way out into the sunshine again, they strolled back along the garden path, out through the iron gates into the island's open grounds.

'We will go this way and I will endeavour to tell you a little of the history of this place,' Henri said. 'The original fortified monastery that literally has *les pieds dans la mer* – feet in the sea – is on this side of the island.'

Leaving the abbey behind them, they set off along the footpath that wound its way around the island. As they approached the recently renovated fortress, Mattie said, 'My dog, Bert, would love this place. He'd be right at home with the shingle beach and as for the sea, he'd be in his element.' She watched the gently lapping water.

Looking at the steep steps leading up to the fortified monastery entrance, Mattie decided the view from the top might be wonderful but she'd settle for the view from ground level.

'You go ahead,' she said. 'I'm not good with heights.'

'Sure? The view is well worth the climb.'

'I'm sure it is but I'll settle for staying on terra firma. The view's not so bad from here anyway.'

'I'll give you a wave from the top, then. Don't wander too far while I'm gone.'

Mattie perched on the small wall above a collection of rocks on the shoreline and drank in the silence, thinking about and waiting for Henri. In seventy-two hours they would be going their separate ways. Back to different lives. He'd been an ideal holiday companion. She would miss him when they said their goodbyes in Nice and she flew home to England.

The whole of her holiday had turned out – with Henri's help – to be rather wonderful. And after that soul-stirring experience in the abbey she was more than ready to face the real world again next week.

When Henri rejoined her, they began to walk with the ease of old friends, companionably around the island. As they strolled, Henri pointed out various landmarks and told Mattie a couple of anecdotes about his childhood.

She frowned as Henri stopped to point out a World War II gun emplacement.

'That is wrong on so many counts,' she said, staring at it and declining to examine it close up. 'What on earth is something like that doing on a religious island?'

'The islands, like the rest of this coast, were occupied by the Germans and the Italians during the war. It was hard down here during those years.'

'Yes, but surely it should have been dismantled by now,' Mattie protested. 'It's no longer needed and it is so at odds with what the island represents.'

'For me it is a symbol of my childhood and reminds me of my grandfather who was in the resistance,' he said quietly. 'I wouldn't like to see it removed. To me it would be a betrayal of those hard times we endured.' Henri was silent for a moment.

'The tender will be arriving soon to take us back to the ship,' Mattie said, breaking the silence. 'I think we'd better make our way to the quay.'

They were both quiet as they made their way past the vineyards where several monks could be seen tending the vines that would produce the abbey's world-famous wines and liqueurs later in the year.

Mattie, uncomfortable with the silence that stretched between them, sighed and tried to explain. 'Henri, I'm sorry if I've upset you. I've enjoyed today and thank you for all the local knowledge. It's just that....' She hesitated before shaking her head and adding: 'No. Sorry. I refuse to spoil the day by talking about the war.'

Katie stayed on at the shop the next evening, planning to get to grips with a final sort-out of the attic room, arranging her new stuff and making up her material from the auction into cushions and curtains, ready to move in when Mattie returned next week.

Leo may have been against her moving in but she was looking forward to having her own space again. It had been fun staying with Mattie but it wasn't her home like this would be. She knew Mattie wouldn't object to her having friends to stay but somehow she couldn't see Patrick in the cottage. Once she'd moved in she'd arrange the flat-warming party she'd promised Lara – and invite Patrick to stay for the weekend.

She was downstairs in the clubroom threading the sewing machine with cotton ready to sew the curtains she'd cut out of the Toile de Jouy material she'd been delighted to discover in the parcel of material, when her mobile rang.

'Hi. Fancy a trip up-river?' Leo asked.

'Sounds a nice idea but I'm busy,' Katie said. 'I'm making curtains with that material I bought.'

'Be raining tomorrow evening,' Leo said. 'You can make curtains then.'

'You trying to delay my move?'

'I think it's unnecessary but it's your decision. Whatever you planned to do tonight, you can do tomorrow evening – when it's raining.'

'You still keep a putt-putt in the Boat Float, then?'

'Putt-putt indeed,' Leo said. 'I'll have you know I've graduated to a fourteen-foot clinker built with an inboard engine. Come on, Katie, it's a lovely evening to be out on the river. It's what life down here is all about.'

Katie looked around. The flat was almost ready and it was a lovely evening. Leo was right. Why live somewhere so beautiful and not take advantage of all it offered? Working to get A Good Yarn up and running, she hadn't been out on the river at all yet.

'OK, you're on.'

'See you at the Boat Float in five. We'll potter up to Old Mill Creek.

'Can I bring Bert?'

'Of course. See you later.'

Leo was waiting for her by the Boat Float ramp, his small day-boat moored up alongside. 'Thought it would be easier for Bert to jump in from here,' he said, helping Katie to step in.

As Leo started the inboard engine and motored out under the low bridge that spanned the embankment, Katie looked back towards the Royal Castle Hotel fronting the quay. 'The town is so much busier these days,' she said.

'Tourist season all year round now,' Leo said, concentrating on steering between some moorings as he made for the centre of the river to go upstream.

Chugging upriver past Sand Quay and the naval college, Katie looked around her at what used to be so familiar but now had a certain unknown quality to it. It did feel good to be out on the river with Leo, though. Just like the old days.

Ten minutes later, Leo turned into Old Mill Creek and was helping her to step ashore.

'It's years since I've been up here,' Katie said. 'We used to come a lot, didn't we?'

'Yep. Anything to get away from the parents and while away a few hours.'

Katie smiled. 'Finding a few hours to while away these days is difficult with the shop.' She glanced at a wicker basket and blanket in the stern of the boat. 'What's that?'

'I brought a picnic,' Leo said.

'You feeding me is becoming a bit of a habit,' Katie said.

'Can you take Bert and the blanket? I'll bring the food. I just need to secure the boat first,' Leo said. 'We've got an hour or so before the tide turns and we have to make a move.'

Bert bounded out of the boat and was soon happily sniffing his way around the undergrowth that bordered the shore. While Leo secured the boat, Katie wandered along the shore and found the perfect picnic spot.

As she spread the blanket on the ground Leo joined her and unpacked the wicker basket. A couple of pasties – heated through and wrapped in foil to keep them warm – and two individual containers that Katie guessed contained raspberries and cream. There was also a bottle of red wine and two glasses.

'No dessert until you've eaten your pasty,' Leo said. 'So, seen anything of Ron or the other Blackawton relatives?'

Katie shook her head. 'No, thankfully. Probably realized they were wasting their time. I'm sure Mattie can do what she likes with A Good Yarn.'

'Hope so,' Leo said thoughtfully. 'You can never be sure, though, with the Blackawton relatives. They're a devious bunch.'

'Never been able to work out the connection to you and Mattie,' Katie said.

'We're all related somehow through a rogue Victorian uncle,' Leo shrugged. 'Not really sure how, myself. It's so complicated. You ready for dessert?' he added, handing her a container and spoon.

'You're spoiling me. Thank you.' Katie glanced around.

'We've had a few picnics here, haven't we?' There had been quite a gang of them in pre-college days and lots of summer evenings had been spent out on the river. Lara, having access to dinghies from her family's boatyard, would motor downriver and pick everybody up. Old Mill Creek had a been a favourite destination and they'd all jump out with their various bits of bounty – wine, cheese, cold sausages along with anything else unsuspecting family fridges had yielded. One of the boys had once brought a packet of roll-your-own tobacco. Katie had taken one puff and it had put her off smoking for life.

'Remember how we used to search for the folly that was supposedly built down here by a lovelorn lord of the manor?'

'Such a romantic idea – an eighteenth-century meeting place for star-crossed lovers.' Katie laughed. 'We were convinced it contained lost treasure of some description too. We never did find it though, did we?' she added, as Leo poured the last of the wine into their glasses.

'No. I suspect the lost-treasure ploy was a local myth dreamt up by various grown-ups to keep us occupied and out of the way,' Leo said. 'Access must have been by boat or a mile down the steep lane by horseback. Both methods would have been difficult then – almost impossible for a woman on her own.'

'Why are you always so practical?' Katie sighed. 'Can't you just imagine a lovers' tryst happening down here?'

'Oh, I can imagine it. But even these days, it would take a special kind of woman to make it a reality,' he said, staring at her silently for several seconds before turning away.

'Right, time to head back. Tide is on the turn.' He began to throw the remains of their picnic into the basket.

It was peaceful on the river as they made their way back down to town. Katie, happy to sit and watch the lights coming on all over town, wished she'd thought to bring a pullover. It was cold out on the water now that the sun had gone down.

'Put the blanket around you,' Leo said, noticing her shiver and pushing the picnic hamper towards her. As she pulled it over her shoulders the strains of *Old MacDonald had a Farm* began to fill the air. Embarrassed, Katie began to search her bag.

'What on earth?' Leo said.

'It's my phone. After what you said about me not hearing it, I decided to go for a totally different ringtone that would . . . oh, one that would catch my attention,' Katie said, lifting her phone from the depths of her bag and pressing the button.

'Well, that's certainly different,' Leo laughed.

'Patrick. Hi, how lovely to hear from you,' Katie said. 'I'm fine. You?'

Leo leant forward and pressed something on the inboard motor and the boat slowed its movement through the water as the regular thump, thump of the engine grew quieter. Pointedly Leo turned his gaze away from Katie and concentrated on steering between the lines of moored boats.

'Thanks for the invite,' Katie said, before falling silent and listening to Patrick. Minutes passed before she managed to interrupt him. 'Patrick, please listen to me. I doubt that there is any way I can make it on that date so please find someone else to take. I honestly don't mind. No, I don't need time to think about it. OK – you too.' She closed her phone down.

'What does he want now?'

'Not that it's any of your business,' Katie said. 'He wants me to attend a black-tie do with him in June. Doesn't seem to understand I live a different life now and can't just drop everything and swan off to posh hotels.'

'Would you go if you could? I'm sure Trisha and Mattie between them could manage the shop for a couple of days.'

'No.' Katie shook her head emphatically. 'I loved my job but I never did like all those glitzy, "aren't we clever" pat-on-the-back industry dos that the media seems to go in for.'

'So he hasn't dumped you completely, then?'

'No.' Katie pointedly turned her back on him. She had no intention of discussing her relationship with Patrick with Leo.

Leo shrugged and, leaning forward, moved the throttle on the engine. Responding to the increased power, the boat began to move quickly through the water and within minutes they were approaching the Boat Float and heading under the bridge.

Leo pulled up alongside the ramp and helped Katie out before handing her Bert's lead and waiting for the dog to jump out.

'Want a hand tying up?' Katie asked.

Leo shook his head. 'No need.'

'Would you like a coffee back at the cottage?'

'Have to get back to the farm.'

'Well I'll be off, then,' Katie said. 'Thanks for the picnic and everything.'

'You're welcome. I'll see you in the week. Ciao,' and expertly Leo manoeuvred the boat away from the ramp towards his usual mooring place.

'Ciao.' Katie shortened Bert's lead and began to walk towards home. If Leo was going to sulk because she'd taken a phone call from Patrick, that was his problem but Patrick's phone call had spoilt what had been a lovely evening.

THIRTEEN

'Oh, I'm going to buy one of these,' Mattie said, laughing and pointing to a stand of umbrellas outside a souvenir shop in one of the ancient streets near Monaco Palace. 'I've been promising myself a new one for ages.'

'Which one would you like?' Henri said.

'The scarlet one that says, "It never rains in Monte Carlo,"' Mattie said.

Despite Mattie's protest Henri insisted on buying the umbrella for her. 'A souvenir of your first cruise and your first visit to France,' he said. 'I hope it doesn't get too much use in Devon. And don't forget – it's unlucky to open it indoors.'

'Thank you, Henri,' Mattie said. 'Now you're making me feel guilty. I haven't thought of buying you a souvenir. I know! I'll treat you to lunch.'

'We've got time to visit the cathedral first,' Henri said.

The two of them were on their last sightseeing trip of the cruise. Tomorrow the ship would dock in Nice and they would say their farewells. Sitting at a table for two, tucked away in a discreet corner of a small restaurant, Mattie watched Henri study the menu and thought how comfortable she was with him.

She couldn't remember a time when she'd been so relaxed with a man, apart from Michael, of course, and he didn't count. Growing up after the war and already too old to appreciate the swinging sixties when they arrived, she'd had few boyfriends. Mother had seen to that, keeping her busy and tied to the shop. When, at twenty-four, she'd met Bernard – a lecturer at the college – Mother had swiftly interfered and shown him the door. 'Not our type,' she'd informed Mattie and that had been that.

By her thirtieth birthday, she'd given up all hope of meeting anyone else and buried deep her dream of having children. She was so lucky to have been asked to be Katie's godmother. For years now she'd regarded Katie as her surrogate daughter and so much more than just a goddaughter.

Mattie picked up the glass of ice-cold rosé an attentive waiter had poured for her and said, 'Santé.'

As they clicked their glasses she said, 'Henri, I need to thank you for making this holiday so special for me, and to say a proper thank-you for the other day on St Honorat. I shall always remember visiting the island with you. It's a truly special place.'

She paused as Henri looked at her intently. 'I'm sorry about my reaction to the gun emplacement. The wounds of that time still run deep in me – and I suspect in you too. The part of Devon I live in was commandeered during the war and occupied, mainly by the American forces. I was only a child at the time but my life changed for ever because of their presence.'

As Henri put his glass down on the table, he closed his

eyes as though trying to suppress his emotions. 'Did you starve during those years?' he asked in a low voice. 'With the Americans around with their black-market goodies, I doubt it. Could you still move around freely? Permission to travel five miles up the road was needed here – and rarely given. Did you see your friend hollow-eyed and afraid when their father disappeared overnight – never to be seen again? Did you?' Henri demanded.

Mattie, startled at the ferocity in his voice, flinched. 'No,' she whispered. 'My sister died as a result of the American occupancy.'

'For that, I am truly sorry,' Henri said. 'But for me and thousands of others, the Americans and the British saved my life. I can never think of that without humble gratitude.'

Henri stared at Mattie without speaking for several seconds. 'Mattie, my dear, I don't know what happened to you or your sister during the war, but don't you think it's time you looked at the bigger picture? Accept what happened in the past and simply thank God you're alive and living in a free society?'

Mattie, stunned into silence by the vehemence behind Henri's words, bit her lip. Henri's hand reached across the table to gently take hold of hers.

'The legacy of war lingers on in all of us,' he continued, 'but you have to try and overcome all these negative memories. It is hurting and spoiling your life. I'm sure your sister would urge you to let go and remember the happy times.'

Mattie sighed. 'I know you're right but it is difficult. I'm not sure I can. Maybe I've left it too late.' She choked back the tears that were threatening to fall.

'It's never too late. Take small steps,' Henri said. 'Maybe talk to the American film company when you return?'

Mattie nodded. 'I could do that, I suppose.'

'One step at a time. They don't have to be enormous, just big enough to help move you forward into accepting the past and enjoying the rest of your life.'

'I'll do my best,' Mattie said, conscious that Henri was still holding her hand.

'*Bon!*' Henri squeezed her hand gently. 'I shall visit and make sure you do.'

'Oh. You will?'

'*Oui* – if you don't mind?'

Mattie shook her head. 'I think it's a wonderful idea. I shall enjoy showing you my country.'

Katie placed three pink roses she'd cut from the early-flowering bush that Mattie was fond of in a small vase and placed it on the table. A perfect centrepiece for the welcome home supper.

Moving into the kitchen, she checked that supper was cooking on schedule. Another twenty minutes and it would be ready. Hopefully Leo would have returned by then with Mattie.

Minutes later, Bert began to whimper before rushing to scratch determinedly at the front door. Katie opened the door and laughed as Bert pushed past her and up the path to greet Mattie and Leo.

'Welcome home. You look wonderful,' Katie said, hugging Mattie. 'Love your hair. You've obviously had a good time.'

'I did,' Mattie managed to say before she was almost

bowled over by Bert. 'I guess somebody missed me, then,' she said, stroking him.

'I'll take your cases up to your room,' Leo said.

'Leave the smaller one – there are presents in there. And a bottle of wine to go with our meal,' Mattie said. 'Leo tells me you've had problems at the shop. I shall have to have words with cousin Ron.'

Katie sighed. 'Leo, we agreed not to mention the break-in to Mattie tonight. Besides we don't know for sure Ron is involved.'

'Sorry,' Leo shrugged. 'It just slipped out.'

'Are the Americans still in town?' Mattie asked.

'Yes. They've filmed the shop and are waiting for your go-ahead to use it,' Katie said.

'Do you think they'd still be interested in talking to me? Not that I remember a great deal,' Mattie said.

'Noah would be delighted, I'm sure,' Katie said. 'Friendly American on board ship, then?'

'No. It was Henri.'

Katie raised her eyebrows. 'Henri?'

'A fellow passenger. He's planning to visit soon so you'll get to meet him.'

Katie waited for Mattie to say more. When she didn't, she said, 'So tell us about the cruise. Did you make many friends on board? Was the food good? Did you play roulette in the Monte Carlo Casino? Did you like France?'

'Yes. Yes. No. My absolute favourite place was a tiny island off the coast at Cannes that Henri and I visited together.'

Over dinner Mattie continued to regale Katie and Leo with tales of her holiday and how much she'd enjoyed the cruise. She blushed as she admitted meeting Henri had been the highlight of her holiday.

'Henri told me about his childhood during the war, living in Cannes, which was occupied by the Germans. The war I lived through here was far removed from the one he experienced. His war was much harder and far more traumatic than mine.' Mattie fiddled with her wine glass.

'Henri made me think about things and I've realized what a foolish old woman I've become.'

Katie and Leo waited.

'I promised Henri that I would start to try to put things into perspective. He suggested talking to the Americans would be a good start.'

Mattie stood up and pushed her chair back. 'Five minutes. I need to fetch something from my room.'

'Can I help?' Leo said.

Mattie shook her head. 'No. Won't be a moment.'

Katie busied herself clearing the table and Leo drank his wine while they waited for Mattie to return downstairs, both wondering what she'd gone to fetch.

When she returned, she was holding a large envelope and an unframed black and white photo. 'This is Clara and me taken shortly before the Americans arrived in town.' Mattie handed the photograph to Katie. 'For years I couldn't bear to look at this photo.'

'You can definitely tell you're sisters,' Katie said. 'You look like a younger version of her.'

Mattie smiled. 'Clara was my best friend as well as being my big sister, even though she was six years older. I loved her. Idolized her. I hated my parents for driving her away.'

Carefully, Mattie opened the envelope and gently pulled out a folded piece of paper. 'Clara wrote to me regularly after she left. This is the last letter she sent to me from Bridgewater, where she was living. In it she says she misses Hal so much she can't bear the thought of coming back here and having constant reminders of him in places where they'd been so happy together.'

The tears began to course down Mattie's cheeks. 'So, she'd decided to accept a kind friend's invitation and go abroad to make a new life for herself. She was sorry she couldn't tell me where she was going and would be unable to see me before she left but she promised she'd write when she was settled and I was to go for a visit when I was old enough.'

Mattie picked up a faded, fragile newspaper cutting. 'My letter arrived the day after I was told she'd died. According to this newspaper report, she'd just posted a letter when an out-of-control car ploughed into her and she was killed instantly. But my parents didn't tell me that at the time. They simply said Clara was dead. They wouldn't even let me go to the funeral. Said I was too young.'

Mattie looked at Katie and Leo with grief-stricken eyes. 'It was years before I found out the truth about her death. Ever since, I've blamed myself. If only she hadn't gone that particular morning to post that letter to me I believe she would still be alive.'

Katie handed her a tissue before placing a comforting arm around Mattie's shoulders.

'Oh, Mattie. You mustn't. There is no way you can blame yourself. It was simply a tragic accident.'

Wiping the tears away, Mattie sighed. 'I know it's totally illogical, but I've always blamed the Americans too. That's why I've never wanted anything to do with them. If they'd never been billeted down here, she would have lived. It was loving and losing Hal that really killed Clara.'

Katie was silent. It was Leo who spoke quietly. 'Mattie, I think you have to accept all this is in the past and let it go. You have nothing to blame yourself for. It was Clara's decision to leave home. I know you feel your parents drove her to it,' he said, holding up his hand as Mattie went to speak, 'but at the end of the day it was Clara's decision to leave.' Gently Leo took Mattie's hand and stroked it.

'You're fond of saying the past is the past, leave it alone – but until you let the shadows of Clara's life go out of yours, you'll never be truly happy.'

'You sound like Henri,' Mattie said, smiling through her tears.

'Maybe the two of us are right?' Leo said as he hugged her. 'Try it? Let go of what you can't change.'

Mattie bit her lip as she nodded. 'I will try. Starting next week.' She looked at them tearfully. 'It's the anniversary of Clara's death. Will you both come to the cemetery with me?'

Two evenings later, Mattie – clutching a bunch of lilies – led Katie and Leo through Longcross Cemetery towards the corner where Clara was buried.

Katie followed slowly. This was the first time she'd been here since her grandmother had died. Perhaps she should have brought flowers of her own? Now that she was back living down here it would be easy to visit regularly. She vaguely remembered it being somewhere in the middle of the cemetery. She'd ask Mattie later if she knew where Grandma Margaret's grave was.

Every grave they passed seemed to bear a familiar local name, families that had played their part in the history of her home town. They were all there: Widdicombes, Mitchelmores, Peakes, Folletts, Teagues. Katie stopped to look at that one.

'Katharine Teague. Aged 30. Died 1920. Taken from us too soon.' Katie shivered. A distant relative? How had her namesake died?

Leo noticed her shiver. 'Don't like cemeteries?'

Katie shook her head. 'No. It's not that. I quite like the stillness. The feeling of . . . I'm not sure what actually, but the atmosphere here is peaceful and strangely comforting. It was seeing my name staring back at me from a tombstone.' She pointed to the inscription. 'I wonder how she died, what kind of life she led compared to mine.' Katie sighed. 'I guess I'll never know.'

'We'd better catch Mattie up,' Leo said.

The plot Mattie finally stopped in front of was unadorned, its grass neatly mowed. A small headstone inscribed with the bald facts 'Clara Cranford 1926–1945'. No memorial phrase, no 'Loving daughter', no 'Beloved sister', no 'RIP'.

The graves around it were ornate in comparison: marble cherubs and angels, loving words on the gravestones, fresh flowers and potted plants. Loving tributes to much-missed loved ones.

'My parents were never ones to make a big show,' Mattie said. 'I think they surpassed themselves with the negativity of Clara's grave.'

She was silent for a moment. 'They told me she'd died but didn't tell me anything more. They didn't even tell me when the funeral was and it was nearly a year before I discovered she was buried here.'

Carefully Mattie placed the lilies at the head of the grave. 'I spent a lot of time here after that, talking to Clara. Telling her how angry I was with her for leaving me, how I hated our parents. Promising when I was grown up and had some money I'd have the words 'My Beloved Sister' added to the headstone. But, shamefully, I never have.'

Gently Katie touched her arm. 'The grave is obviously cared for.'

Mattie nodded. 'It's easy to pay for its maintenance and flowers once a year. I haven't been coming personally for a long time. Which makes me as bad as my parents. I've neglected Clara and written her life off as much as they ever did.' She brushed a tear away.

'I'm sure it's not too late to have a new inscription done,' Katie said. 'If you feel you still want to.'

Mattie looked at her. 'You're right, and I do. If they know nothing else about her, people should know Clara was a loving sister.'

'There's a stonemason out Totnes way,' Leo said. 'Work out what you want to put and I'll get the stone over to them.'

FOURTEEN

'You've made this look lovely,' Mattie said, standing in the attic room. 'I do wish, though, you didn't feel you have to move out.'

'Mattie, I know I don't have to,' Katie said, giving her a hug. 'But we're both used to having our own space, our own things around. Besides, having someone living here will be better security – despite what Leo says.'

Absently, Mattie fingered one of the cushion covers which Katie had made with the William Morris material she'd been delighted to find in the bundle from the auction. 'You won't move for a few days yet, will you? I shall miss you when you go.'

'Still waiting for the mattress to arrive,' Katie said. 'So you've got me for a bit longer yet. Can't decide whether to have my flat-warming party before or wait until I'm finally in residence. Lara and Dexter are keen to come for that.'

'I look forward to it,' Mattie said. 'Right, if you don't need my help in the shop today, I think I'll go to Torquay.'

Later that morning, Katie was in the clubroom – sorting out publicity for Worldwide Knit in Public Day for the club members to distribute – when Noah Jnr and Vicky arrived, hoping to see Mattie.

'Sorry, she's gone to Torquay for the day,' Katie said. 'Can I give her a message?'

'She's invited us for Sunday tea,' Vicky said. 'But something has come up and we both have to go up to Somerset in the morning and then I'm flying back to the States. Bro here won't get back down here until late on Sunday, so Dad will be coming on his own.'

'Shame. Mattie was looking forward to meeting you – now she's found her sense-of-humour button regarding you Americans,' Katie smiled.

'I'm hoping my grandmother will come back with me for a holiday so maybe we can arrange another time. I'm sure they'll get on,' Vicky said. 'I think they're about the same age.'

As Katie closed the shop that evening, Leo arrived carrying a large box.

'Mattie said you were working down here every evening this week so I've come to give you a hand.'

'There's no need, honestly. You've done so much for me already. Besides, don't you have things to do? People to see? A farm to run?'

'Not tonight. This evening I'm all yours. I shall, of course, continue to point out the error of you leaving Mattie's and living above the shop.'

'Nothing to do with you, Leo – where I live. What's in the parcel?'

'Burglar alarm,' Leo said. 'I'll fit it for you later. Now let's see what you've been doing to the sitting room.'

Katie sighed and, giving in to the inevitable, followed Leo up the narrow stairs to the attic.

'You've done a good job up here,' Leo said. 'No curtains yet?'

'Was planning to put the rail up this evening,' Katie said.

'I'll do it,' Leo said.Knowing it was useless to argue with him, Katie handed him the drill and watched as he set the ladder up.

'Have you found anything out about the break-in?' she asked, watching as he expertly drilled holes for the screws.

'Only that there are a few plans floating around to update the town. Nothing to implicate Ron,' Leo said. 'Think Mattie wants me to take her over to Blackawton later this week to tackle Ron in person and see what we can learn.'

'What sort of plans?'

'The usual sort. But like I said – nothing to implicate Ron. Incomers wanting to change things. Plus the normal claptrap from the council about making the amenities more user-friendly for the tourists.'

'If Ron is involved, he's not likely to talk to you though, is he?' Katie said.

'Knowing that Mattie suspects him may push him into a corner and he'll stop for fear of the police being involved. We can but hope,' Leo said. 'How is she now?'

'I think we owe this Henri a big thank-you. He clearly made quite an impression on her,' Katie said. 'I was worried after her breakdown last week but she's happier since our cemetery visit. It seems to have kick-started her into action.'

'Right, ready for the rail now. Pass it up. What sort of action?'

'She's busy sorting out stuff her parents left in the attic,' Katie said. 'Apparently there are some old family photos taken before the Americans arrived in 1943 and took over the college as their HQ for Operation Overlord. Says she wants to show them to the Empreys.'

'Is that level?' Leo said, stepping off the ladder to look at the rail.

Katie nodded. 'Perfect.'

Leo dragged the ladder across to the next window.

'Mattie showed me a photo of Clara and your dad yesterday, taken out at the castle with their parents before the war,' Katie said, fetching the second rail for him. 'I keep forgetting her parents were your grandparents. Old Ma Cranford was pretty scary to me – was she a nice granny?'

Leo began making the holes for the second curtain rail.

'I think she was nicer to me and Josh than she ever was to Dad and Mattie. The real tyrant was Great-grandmother Luttrell. She was a Victorian matriarch down to her fingertips!'

'I don't remember her.'

'No reason you should. She wasn't your great-gran. Besides, I was only about six when she died so you could only have been four or five.'

Leo screwed the second rail into position. 'According to Dad, it's the Luttrell side that is responsible for the Ron connection.'

'Mattie said there was a rogue Luttrell ancestor that links you and the Blackawton cousins.'

Leo shrugged. 'Family history is not really my scene. I'm

much more interested in the future – my future,' he said, glancing at Katie.

'I'm starting to be fascinated by it all,' Katie said.

'Right. Curtain rails are ready,' Leo said. 'While you hang the curtains, I'm going to fit the burglar alarm downstairs.'

'Leo, it's not necessary,' Katie protested.

'It's non-negotiable. It's going up,' Leo said.

'OK,' Katie said, realizing there was nothing she could do to change Leo's mind. 'I'll come down and make us some coffee once I've finished up here.'

When she got downstairs with the coffee, Leo was outside drilling a hole to pull some wire through.

'Can you get the ladder and pull this through, please?' he said. 'Be careful – don't want you falling off. I remember the last time I asked you to climb a ladder.'

'Leo, I was fifteen,' Katie said, standing the ladder against the wall and carefully climbing a few rungs to reach the hole where the wire would appear. She'd never admit it to Leo but she didn't like ladders. Her sense of balance seemed to desert her when she stood on the first rung of one.

'Anyway, that wasn't a proper ladder. It was an old mooring ladder you'd got from somewhere and fixed to the trunk of a tree-house you'd built in the garden. It wasn't so much that I fell off – more that the whole thing collapsed under me.' And scared me for life, she thought.

'Perfectly good ladder. You were just too heavy for it. Can you see the wire yet?'

Katie bit back a retort about her weight, made a grab for the wire, which was tantalisingly out of reach – and fell off the ladder, ending in a crumbled heap on the floor.

'Tiggy, I knew I shouldn't have asked you to help,' Leo said, rushing in. 'You're a complete liability where ladders are concerned. Are you all right?' Tenderly he put his arm around her and lifted her to her feet, holding her while he regarded her anxiously. 'Where do you hurt? Ankle? Arm? Back? Where?'

'I'm OK,' Katie said. 'Bit shaken but don't think I've broken anything.'

'Thank goodness,' Leo said, still holding her.

'You can let me go now,' Katie said. 'I'm not about to fall over.'

There was a pause of several seconds before Leo said quietly, 'The thing is, Tiggy, I don't want to let you go ever again.'

As Katie stared at him, shocked at the intensity in his voice, he pulled her against him and placed a gentle kiss on her lips. 'Oh, Tiggy,' he murmured, taking his lips away from her. 'I've wanted to do that for so long.'

Katie, surprised at the feelings Leo's gentle kiss had aroused in her, stirred in his arms and as his lips met hers for the second time, she responded to the delicious intimacy of his kiss.

A loud knocking on the shop door made them both jump and draw apart.

'Who the devil?' Leo muttered. 'Stay here. I'll go.'

Katie took several deep breaths to calm herself down. Whoever was at the door and whatever happened next, she doubted things between her and Leo could ever be the same again.

'Tiggy, can you come here, please?' Leo called. 'Someone here to see you.'

'Bit late for visitors, isn't it?' Katie said as she went through to the shop and stopped in shock.

'Patrick. What on earth are you doing here?'

FIFTEEN

'Coffee?'

'I'd prefer wine.'

'No can do. Haven't moved in yet so there's none here,' Katie said, filling the kettle and flicking the switch.

'Suppose that means there's nothing to go with the coffee?'

Katie shook her head. 'Got it in one. You'll have to eat at the hotel.'

'I was hoping to stay with you,' Patrick said.

Katie shook her head again. 'Sorry. I'm still living at Mattie's and there's no bed here. You'd better ring the Castle Hotel and hope they've got a vacancy.' Honestly, did he really expect to leap straight into her bed after the sulking of the past weeks?

Patrick took out his iPhone and scrolled through his address book.

'You know the hotel number?' Katie said.

Patrick nodded, pressing his screen. 'You know me. Boy scout ready for anything. Ah, hi,' he said. 'Patrick Tegwen here. Just wanted to confirm my booking for this evening. I've been delayed but should be with you soon. Thanks.'

He caught the expression on Katie's face as he closed his phone. 'What?'

'Nothing,' Katie said. 'Just that you're unbelievable. I still don't understand why you're here, though,' she said, spooning coffee into the cafetière.

'I've got a new location to check out near Plymouth tomorrow, so I thought I'd break the journey and see my girlfriend. Not that you seem that pleased to see me. Not even a welcoming kiss.'

'Of course I'm pleased to see you,' Katie said, moving across to him. 'I'm surprised, that's all.' She reached up to kiss him. 'You've always said you're too busy when I've mentioned coming for a visit.'

'There's a film crew here in town I'm rather keen to meet up with,' Patrick added, before kissing her back and nuzzling her neck. 'Are you sure you won't come back to the hotel?'

Katie pulled back and looked at him. She might have guessed Patrick wouldn't be here just to see her. 'Do you mean the Empreys?'

'You know them? Great, you can help me get them on board,' Patrick said. 'Persuade them to sell me the English rights to this World War Two documentary they're filming.'

'I don't think so, Patrick. I'm completely out of touch these days with the business.' She moved out of the circle of his arms and switched off the kettle.

Patrick shrugged. 'Pity. So, who's the country bumpkin who was here earlier?'

'Less of the country bumpkin,' Katie said, pouring the water on to the coffee. 'Leo is anything but. And you know very well who he is – I introduced you.' And wasn't that embarrassing she thought, plunging the cafetière strainer down.

The two men had touched knuckles more than shaken hands and Leo had left without another word. Katie had called out, 'Thanks for your help this evening' but he'd merely raised his hand in acknowledgement and kept walking. Katie had sighed inwardly. This wasn't the way she'd planned on introducing the two men to each other. She'd hoped they'd get on, instead of clearly loathing each other on sight.

'He was a tad protective of you when I told him who I was,' Patrick said. 'Almost as though he has a prior claim over you?'

'Leo and I grew up together. He's always looked out for me like a big brother,' Katie said, trying not to think about the way Leo had kissed her earlier. Definitely no brotherly feelings involved there.

'Besides, he's convinced that long-distance relationships are doomed to failure and that you'd dumped me without bothering to tell me.' Katie poured the coffee before looking at Patrick. 'And let's face it. I've barely heard from you since I've been down here. Let's take this upstairs.'

'I've been busy. You know how hectic it can get,' Patrick said, following her up to the attic room.

'You could still have replied to my texts,' Katie said, handing him his coffee.

Patrick moved across to look out of the window before he answered. 'Leo is right about long-distance relationships being difficult,' he said, 'which is one of the reasons I'm here now. We need to talk.'

Katie sipped her coffee and waited.

'But I'd rather do it when we've got more time – and I'm not so hungry.'

'You could always phone for a pizza,' Katie said.

Patrick pulled a face. 'You know how I feel about pizzas. I've got a better idea. Why don't we just go to the hotel and have dinner together. You could always stay with me after-wards – I've booked a double room.' Patrick looked at her hopefully. 'Then tomorrow you can show me the local sights.'

'Patrick, I'm working all day tomorrow. Any sightseeing you do will have to be alone. Besides, you just said you have to check out a new location.'

'You could come and show me the way to Plymouth, no? OK, I get the message. But we do have to talk and it's going to take more than five minutes.'

Patrick drained his coffee. 'OK, here's the plan. I'll take myself off to the hotel. Go to Plymouth tomorrow, do the biz, be back here the next day. We'll talk then.'

'Can't you at least give me a clue what this is all about?'

Patrick shook his head. 'It'll keep for another few hours. But I know you'll like it. Right, I'd better go and book into the Castle. Hope their dining room doesn't close early.'

'I'll walk there with you,' Katie said.

'Fancy a nightcap before you go?' he asked at the entrance.

Katie shook her head. 'No, thanks. I'll see you when you get back from Plymouth.' She leant forward and kissed him goodnight before turning and making her way back to Above Town.

She wished Patrick had come straight out with whatever he wanted to talk to her about, instead of being mysterious.

Maybe he thought the anticipation would increase the chances of her agreeing to whatever it was. It was typical of Patrick to turn up and expect her to be immediately available to him.

This 'thing' he wanted to talk about was probably just another job offer which she would turn down and he'd tell her again she was being stupid before going back to Bristol and ignoring her for weeks on end. Sighing, she opened the cottage gate. She was beginning to feel that her relationship with Patrick was doomed.

Sixteen

Mattie heard the gentle plop of letters on the front doormat as she finished lunch and made herself a coffee. Quickly checking through the bills and junk mail, she was irrationally pleased to see a letter with a Parisian postmark. Taking it and her coffee out to sit at the wrought-iron table under the blossom of the magnolia tree, she settled down to read it.

Henri wrote English as well as he spoke it and Mattie could hear his voice in her head as she read, thanking her for a wonderful holiday, trusting she'd had a safe journey home and telling her he planned to visit soon – in about ten days if that was OK and could she please recommend some-where for him to stay.

Thoughtfully Mattie stared out across the river and came to a decision. Fetching her writing folder and a pen she replied to Henri, telling him the only place she could confidently recommend was her cottage and that she expected him to stay with her, no argument. A few more sentences about how much she was looking forward to seeing him again and she hesitated over her signature before settling on 'Yours affectionately, Mattie'. She'd post the letter on her way to the shop to meet Leo – who was driving her out to see Ron.

Katie was serving a customer when she arrived and there was no sign of Leo. Rather than stand around watching Katie, Mattie made her way to the clubroom to sit and wait. A man aimlessly flicking through a magazine glanced up at her and smiled.

'Ah, you must be Patrick,' Mattie said, remembering how agitated Katie had been the night he'd arrived. 'Katie's ex-boss.'

'Rather more than just an ex-boss,' Patrick said. 'Close friend too. You must be Mattie,' he added, holding out his hand. 'The reason Katie came home to bury herself.'

Reluctantly Mattie shook his hand. She'd decided before she'd even met Patrick she wasn't going to like him and his last comment confirmed it.

'Katie came home because she wanted to. I didn't make her.'

Patrick shrugged. 'Whatever. It's a nice enough place but I know Katie will be restless and want to move back to the city in – oh, I give it another six months at the most. Less, if I have anything to do with it. Already got a job lined up for her the minute she wants it.'

Mattie stared at him. 'How long exactly are you planning to stay?'

'Got a spot of business to see to down here and a couple of days' annual leave to use up so....' Patrick shrugged again. 'A few days at least while I try to talk some sense into Katie. Make her an offer she can't refuse.'

'I see you two have introduced yourselves,' Katie said, walking into the clubroom at that moment. 'You haven't told me anything yet about this offer I can't refuse,' she added, turning to Patrick.

'Tell you later. Over dinner?'

Katie shook her head. 'I'm busy later. In fact, I'm busy now so why don't you go and let me get on with some work? I've told you I can't just drop everything on a whim – or because you insist.' She was surprised at how cross she still felt over his unexpected appearance and demands for her time.

Patrick glanced at his watch. 'Hell, yes. I've got an appointment with the Empreys in about five minutes so I'd better get going.'

The sound of a car horn tooting came in through the window.

'That'll be Leo,' Mattie said. 'I'm off. See you later.' Pointedly ignoring Patrick, she left.

Once settled in Leo's car she slammed the door shut.

'Something the matter?' Leo asked.

'Mr Smoothie's in the shop.'

'Mr Smoothie? Oh, you've met Patrick.'

'He seems to blame me for Katie coming home. But she'd been made redundant – I offered her an opportunity which she accepted.' Mattie sighed. 'I do hope she didn't take it just to please me.'

'Fairly certain she took the shop on because she fancied the challenge,' Leo said.

'He seems confident that he can make her change her mind. He's going to make her an offer.'

'Between us we'll just have to make her an even better offer then, won't we?' Leo said.

'Any ideas how we do that?'

'I'm working on it,' Leo said with a smile. 'So, decided what we're going to say to Ron?'

'Not really. Challenge him about the break-in and the earlier vandalism. See what his reaction is. Not sure what else we can do.'

Mattie sighed. 'I just hope he'll speak to us. It's never been that easy dealing with Ron and the old family agreement always rears its complicated head.'

Leo glanced across at her. 'I thought that agreement was a family myth.'

'Wish it was. All down to dear Grandmother Luttrell. Caused untold problems in the past and continues to do so. The main problem is the clause that gives Ron and his family 40% of any profit on the sale of the shop building.'

Leo whistled. 'That's a lot of money in any century. Can see why Ron wants you to sell up.'

'The thing is, the agreement does finally expire next year. Another twelve months and ownership reverts to me totally . . . to do what I like with.'

Mattie was silent as Leo drove through Blackawton village before turning down the potholed farm lane that led to Ron's farm. 'You'd think he'd tidy the place up a bit,' Leo muttered, looking at the rusting machinery littering the adjoining fields. 'Place is more like a scrapyard than a farm.'

'Ron didn't ever want to be a farmer,' Mattie said. 'As the only son, he inherited the place. He's never worked the place as a proper farm. Now he's looking for yet another handout from the family.'

Ron was on the yard working on an old tractor as they pulled up outside the farmhouse, but made no attempt to greet them. Belatedly he yelled, 'Quiet!' at the Alsatian dog frantically barking at them from his chain by an outbuilding.

'What do you two want?'

'Wanted to talk to you about the shop,' Mattie said. 'See if you know anything about the recent problems we've had.' She stared at Ron and waited.

'Why should I know something about your problems? Like you keep telling me – place ain't nothing to do with me.'

'So you're not trying to make Mattie sell up and share the proceeds with you, then?' Leo said.

'Nothing to do with me. Might want me rightful share of family money but I ain't no criminal.' Ron glowered at them.

'You could be paying someone else to vandalize the shop. This place looks like you could do with the money the property would raise.'

Ron glared at Leo. 'I told you. That ain't nothing to do with me – and you can butt out too. This be between Mattie and me.'

'Ron, don't you think it's time to stop this stupid family feud business?' Mattie said.

'Might be stupid to you,' Ron said. 'You be sitting pretty whatever 'appens. Your lot always did come up smelling of roses. But I've got me rights and that property is one of 'em.'

'Ron, you've had all you're entitled to. After the war your father got thousands to help you all resettle after the evacuation and he still conned the family trustees into lengthening the agreement time limit into the twenty-first century.'

'If your sister had done the right thing and married me, the shop would have been mine anyway.'

Mattie smothered a laugh. 'Clara would never have married you in a million years. She loved Hal not you.'

'So, if you're not behind the break-ins – any idea who might be?' Leo asked.

'Nope. Wouldn't tell you if I did anyway,' Ron said. 'Unless, of course, you made it worth my while.'

'If you're that short of money you could always try working the farm properly,' Leo said. 'Instead of using it as a scrapyard.'

'You can mind your own business – and get off my land.'

Mattie stepped back involuntarily as Ron bent down and picked up a hammer from the toolbox at his feet. Straightening up he glared at them. 'Now bloody well scarper before I set the dog on you.' He turned his back on them and began bashing away at something on the tractor.

'Well, I think I believe him when he says he's not behind the break-ins,' Mattie said as she and Leo returned to the car. 'But I definitely got the feeling he knows more than he's saying.'

'Mmm,' Leo said. 'But we're no closer to finding out who is, exactly. What's this about him and Aunt Clara?'

'Oh, Ron got it into his head she'd make him an ideal wife. It was designed for him to get his hands on the shop. He hadn't reckoned on Clara falling for a GI.'

Mattie looked back at the farmyard where Ron was still

banging away at the tractor. 'I'm blowed if I'm going to be bullied by anybody into selling A Good Yarn, just to give Ron yet another handout. I have too much respect for Clara's memory to do that.'

SEVENTEEN

'Now, you're sure you'll manage? You don't want me to see if Trisha can come in?' Katie looked at Mattie anxiously. 'Ring my mobile if it gets too busy and I'll come back as quickly as I can.'

'Katie, this used to be my shop, remember? I do know how to run it!'

'Sorry,' Katie said. 'I can't think what possessed Patrick to book a table for lunch and simply assume I'd shut up shop.'

'Used to getting his own way, that one,' Mattie said shrewdly. 'Told you what he wants to talk about yet?'

Katie shook her head. 'I haven't had a chance to see him properly yet. I imagine that's what this lunch is all about. Whatever it is, I've a hunch he's going to be disappointed by my reaction.'

'Where is he taking you?'

'The Barge.'

'Well, at least the food will be good. Now, GO!' Mattie said.

Walking along the embankment to where she'd agreed to meet Patrick, Katie thought about what Mattie and Leo had told her about their visit to Ron's. Leo had promised her that if it was Ron, and he caused any more trouble, he would personally make sure he stopped.

Katie smiled as she thought about Leo fighting her battles for her. He'd always protected her like she'd assumed a big brother would. Bossed her around. That was why his kisses the other evening had been so unexpected.

Patrick was waiting by the launch that ferried customers to and from the restaurant barge moored in the middle of the river and raised his hand in greeting as he saw her. Katie smiled and raised her own hand in acknowledgement. She'd forgotten how attractive Patrick was.

Katie felt a stab of guilt as she saw how smart he looked in his white chinos and navy blazer while she was in her normal workday clothes. She banished the guilty thought instantly. Patrick would have to accept the way she was – it was the middle of a working day for her. Unlike him, she wasn't having an away day.

'Patrick, I don't want to be rude but this is going to have to be a quick lunch. I've left Mattie managing A Good Yarn and I don't want to leave her on her own for too long.'

'Have to learn to delegate, Katie. That's what staff are for. An hour of your undivided attention is all I want,' Patrick said. 'Not too much to ask, is it?'

The short journey across the river took barely five minutes and they were soon seated at a table in the main saloon of the barge with a porthole view towards Kingswear. Katie looked around appreciatively. 'This is nice.'

'The Empreys enjoyed it last night,' Patrick said. 'You'll be pleased to hear that I've secured the rights for their documentary. I hear you've played a cameo part in it.'

Katie smiled. 'A very small cameo. Doubt that you'll even have time to recognize me. It was fun to do, though.'

The waiter handed her the menu, pointed out the day's special and left them to decide. Katie declined Patrick's offer of wine. 'Just water, please. I have to work this afternoon. I think I'll have the duck breast salad, please.'

'No starter?'

Katie shook her head. 'No, thanks. Now Patrick, what's this offer you think I won't be able to refuse?'

'First, can I tell you how much I miss you? Really miss having you around.'

Katie looked at him silently and waited.

'I hadn't realized how much you meant to me until you were no longer around,' Patrick continued. 'Katie, come back to Bristol. Stop burying yourself down here. Come back to your old life.'

'Patrick, I have no "old life" to come back to. I was made redundant, remember? So I have no job and nowhere to live up there. Besides, I'm happy I moved back here and took on A Good Yarn.'

'I don't believe that for a minute. You're wasted down here.' Patrick paused before he continued. 'Would a job as executive producer alongside me, a salary of 50K and this, tempt you back?' He reached across the table and placed a small red ring box in her hand and waited for her reaction.

Katie looked at the ring box and then at Patrick, stunned. She hadn't expected this at all. She didn't dare open the box. The kind of job she'd always dreamed of was on offer. Together with a proper commitment, too, from Patrick in the form of what was clearly intended to be an engagement ring.

When she didn't speak, Patrick continued. 'Hugo wants out of the agency so I'm taking over and expanding it. Remember Todd Oaks? Well, he's providing the finance, backing me to the hilt but letting me call all the shots. We made a great team before, Katie, and we can again. Oh, there's something else – I'm about to sign for a two-bedroom flat in Clifton. We'd have a brand new home together too. People would know we were an item.' He squeezed her hand. 'It's all starting to happen for me and I want you to be a part of it. So, Katie, can I ask the waiter to bring the champagne they've put on ice for me and we celebrate in style?'

Katie bit her lip and whispered, 'No, thank you.' Her words hung in the air between them as the waiter returned to take their food order.

'Duck breast salad. Steak,' Patrick told him brusquely before dismissing him with a wave of his hand. Once they were alone again he said, 'Is that a "no" to everything I've offered? Or just to the champagne?'

'Patrick, I'm sorry. You've completely thrown me. I thought there might be a job on offer but this….' She shook her head. 'I can't think straight.'

'You haven't even looked at your ring. It's a diamond solitaire – your secret dream, I know.'

Carefully Katie slid the ring box across the table to Patrick. 'I definitely need time to think about that.'

Silently Patrick picked up the box and replaced it in his pocket before looking at Katie, his face serious.

'You will think about things, then? Promise?'

Katie nodded. 'I promise.'

'Don't take too long though, will you? Need to know where I stand. I've booked the room at the hotel for another couple of nights but I've got to get back at the weekend.'

Katie looked at him. 'Patrick, you say you miss me and it seems you want me back in your life both as a working partner and,' she hesitated before saying, 'as your wife. What you haven't said is that you love me. Do you?'

'What?'

'Love me?' Katie said.

'Wouldn't ask you to marry me if I didn't,' Patrick said. 'Of course I do – and I need you in my life.'

The waiter arrived with their food. Looking at the meal he placed in front of her, Katie's appetite deserted her. There was no way she could eat anything. Pushing her chair back, she stood up.

'Katie, what are you doing?'

'Leaving. Patrick, I'm sorry. I need to go and think. You stay and finish your meal. I'm sorry,' she said again. Banking on the fact that Patrick hated public scenes and wouldn't attempt to stop her, she turned and walked towards the exit, ignoring all the furtive, speculative glances from other diners.

Once the launch had taken her back to shore, Katie walked along the embankment towards A Good Yarn in a daze.

Staring out across the harbour towards the castle, her mind went round and round in circles. Patrick's executive producer role was exactly the kind of job she'd dreamed of obtaining ever since her media course. This time last year she knew she'd have been excited at the opportunity.

And marrying Patrick – that was also something she'd wanted just six months ago. Now? Could she have one without the other or did that go hand in hand with the offer?

Mattie looked at her expectantly as she pushed open the shop door. 'You're back sooner than I expected. Did you accept his offer – whatever it is?'

Katie shook her head. 'Not yet. It's complicated. I've simply agreed to think about it. I'll tell you all about it later. I need to do some work now,' and Katie went to go through to the clubroom, but a determined Mattie blocked the way.

'Wants you to go back, doesn't he?' Mattie said.

Katie sighed and nodded.

'You're actually thinking about it? I thought you were happy running A Good Yarn. Looking forward to living above the shop.'

'Oh, I am,' Katie said. 'I love it. I love being back down here too.'

'Then why are you even thinking about Patrick's offer?'

'Because he's offered me my dream job and....' Katie took a deep breath. 'He wants to marry me. Look, can we please talk about this later?'

On Sunday afternoon, Katie was in Mattie's kitchen helping her prepare tea for Noah Snr and Leo. Bert had been banished to lie in his favourite spot in the garden, from where he sniffed the air appreciatively every so often as the smell of freshly baked scones drifted out of the open kitchen window.

Normally the two of them would have been chatting away companionably about A Good Yarn and the craft club, but not this afternoon. Ever since she'd told Mattie about Patrick's offer, Mattie had been tight-lipped with Katie, desperate to know her decision.

It wasn't fair to her godmother, keeping her in suspense – the future of A Good Yarn was again at stake after all. The thing was, though, Katie knew that if Patrick had made his offer when she was first redundant and before she'd returned down here, she would have jumped at it – at both offers.

The timing was oh so wrong. Things were different now. How could she turn her back on things? But to lose out on her dream job didn't bear thinking about.

'Given your Patrick his answer yet?' Mattie said, breaking the silence. Deftly she emptied a pot of strawberry jam into an old yellow Dartmouth Pottery bowl.

'He's not my Patrick. And no, I haven't given him my answer yet. I'm meeting him later to discuss it.'

'Talked to Leo about it?'

'No. Why should I? Anyway, I haven't seen him since the evening Patrick arrived. I guess he's busy on the farm.' Katie picked up an oven glove. 'I'll get the last batch of scones out, shall I? The pinger's about to go.'

'You've got enough to feed an army here,' she said, carefully placing the scones on the cooling tray.

'Won't last long when Leo and Noah get here,' Mattie said. 'Leo likes his cream tea. Knows what he wants, does Leo,' she added, giving Katie a direct look.

Katie sighed. 'I've always known what I wanted too,' she wanted to say, 'until now. Now I just don't know what to do for the best.'

Leo and Noah Snr arrived together shortly afterwards and, to Katie's relief, Mattie dropped her sullen attitude towards her.

Noah was fascinated by the photographs Mattie had placed on the sideboard for him to see.

Leo picked up one of Ron's farm. 'It looked better in those days than it does now. Is that Clara loading things into the truck?'

Mattie nodded. 'Yes. That one was taken during the evacuation. Ron was in the army by then and Clara helped Old Man Luttrell to move out. Six weeks they had, to get rid of everything – cows, pigs, machinery, feed, hay, chickens.' Mattie laughed. 'We had a couple of chickens here in the garden. Ducks too but they soon flew off to the river. Old Man Luttrell himself was packed off to relatives in Brixham.'

'Dad says he remembers lots of boxes from various people being stored here and in the shop,' Leo said.

'There were,' Mattie said. 'Mainly I remember being very cross when everywhere I liked was made out of bounds to civilians. I couldn't even go riding out at Slapton any more. It did get better, though, when Hal arrived on the scene.'

'Hal?' Noah said.

'Clara's boyfriend. He was an officer in the US Navy, based at the college. Clara got a job as a driver up there and that's how they met.'

Mattie picked up the faded photo Leo had found in the shop to show Noah. 'That's them – and me hanging on.'

'Attractive lady. Did she hope to be a GI bride? I gather there were some from the town. Vicky discovered several names while researching for the documentary. We're hoping to trace them when we get back to the states. See how their lives turned out.'

'My parents insisted Clara was too young. Then Hal was killed in Operation Tiger,' Mattie said. 'I realize now that Clara was heartbroken. At the time I was too young.'

'I'm sorry, ma'am,' Noah said, putting down the photo. 'Katie tells me she died soon afterwards?'

Mattie nodded. 'Yes.'

'So many young men lost their lives at that time,' Noah said. 'Do you know anything about him? Where in the States he was from?'

'Montana. I remember Clara describing the wide-open spaces that Hal had shown her pictures of and the farm they were going to live on together.'

'It's a beautiful State; I know it well. She would have had a good life there. A long way from the coast, though.'

Mattie was silent for a moment, before taking a deep breath and pulling herself together. 'Well, it never happened and it was a long time ago. So many families lost loved ones and had their lives changed forever.'

'That's true,' Noah added. 'My grandmother's twin brother died in the war. She was devastated. His death was apparently the reason she dragged my mother to all the Jane Fonda anti-Vietnam protests. She always had this sad, inconsolable air about her and would never talk about Great-uncle Nathaniel. It's only since she died that we've really learnt anything about her early life.'

He picked up a couple of photos and looked at them again. 'Could I borrow these and make copies? They would make interesting additions to the small exhibition I'm planning.'

'No,' Mattie said instantly, holding out her hand for the photos. 'I'm sorry but these are too personal and too precious to be taken away.'

Noah looked disappointed but didn't press the matter.

'Shall I make the tea?' Katie asked.

'Great idea,' Leo said. 'I'm famished.'

Later, as they sat out on the garden terrace enjoying their cream teas, Noah said, 'I nearly forgot. Vicky has discovered an eighteenth-century family ancestor from the town. One Anne Follett. And now she's managed to persuade my mother to visit this side of the Atlantic for the first time ever.'

'Not just the Pilgrim Fathers linking you to this place, then,' Mattie said, remembering their first ever conversation. 'I'm sorry I've missed meeting Vicky so far. You must bring her and your mother to tea when they arrive.'

The phone rang and Katie went to answer it in the kitchen. Her conversation carried clearly out through the open window.

'Patrick. No, I hadn't forgotten I'm meeting you later. OK. I'll see you at six at the hotel. Yes, I promise I'll give you an answer then. 'Bye.'

Leo looked at her as she returned to the garden. 'I was hoping you'd have supper with me tonight up at the farm,' he said. 'I guess you're going to be busy.'

Katie shook her head. 'No, Patrick has to go back tonight. I'd love to have supper with you,' and she smiled at him happily. 'What time shall I come?'

Before Leo could answer, Mattie looked at her. 'Patrick applying pressure for an answer to his offers, is he? After all, you've had all of two days to decide.'

'What were the offers exactly?' Leo said.

'Oh, you know, Leo,' Mattie said. 'The ones Patrick was confident Katie couldn't refuse.' Leo turned to look at Katie as Mattie continued. 'To return to Bristol for the job of her dreams. Oh, and marriage was also on offer, wasn't it, Katie?

'Is that true?' Leo demanded. 'You have to tell him this evening?'

Katie nodded. 'Yes.'

Leo stood up. 'Katie Teague, say yes to going back and working with Patrick if you must. But agree to marry him and I'll know you have completely taken leave of your senses. Supper tonight is no longer on offer.'

Leo turned to Mattie and Noah. 'Sorry. I've got things to do up at the farm. Thanks for tea, Mattie.' With that, he was gone, the garden gate slamming behind him.

Stunned, Katie looked at Mattie, who shrugged her shoulders at her.

'Like Leo, I hope you aren't about to make the wrong decision,' Mattie said.

'The wrong decision for whom? Me? You? Leo? Patrick? Whatever I decide is going to upset someone, that's for sure, but we're all going to have to accept it and live with it.'

Mattie sighed. 'It's your life – you must do what you want.'

'I intend to,' Katie said. 'I just don't like making other people unhappy in the process.'

Noah cleared his throat. 'Would you like me to leave so you can discuss this privately?'

'No,' Katie said. 'Definitely not. I'm sure Mattie has a lot more to tell you about the evacuation and Operation Tiger. I'll go and make a fresh pot of tea.' Picking up the teapot, Katie hurried indoors to the kitchen, glad to be alone for a few moments.

She might have given Mattie the impression she had decided what to do about Patrick's offers but the truth was, she hadn't. The fact that he would be pressing her for answers in, she glanced at her watch, oh heavens, one and a half hours wasn't at all helpful. As for Leo's outburst, dealing with that would have to wait until after she'd decided which direction she went in from here.

Mattie was explaining to Noah how the evacuation along the coast had changed things for many years when Katie returned to the terrace.

'Not just during the war but for a long time afterwards. I remember how silent and empty it was when I went out to Torcross for the first time after restrictions were lifted. It took years for life to return to normal.'

'I know it took time for the land to be cleared and people to return,' Noah said. 'According to the research we've been doing, some families never came back. Those that did often found vandalized rather than genuinely wrecked homes. Farmers were amongst the first to return, weren't they?'

Mattie nodded. 'I remember Aunt Elsie in tears at the state of her farmhouse in Slapton. Apparently, when they were given permission to return, she and Uncle Tom came over from Paignton to assess the state of things and decided generally it wasn't too bad. When they returned two days later with their possessions the place had been vandalized.

Windows smashed, doors removed and the copper boiler had disappeared. They were devastated.'

'Seems to have happened a lot. Vicky has been researching what happened to the six churches in the evacuation area – Blackawton Church seems to have suffered some of the worse damage.'

'To be honest, Noah, I was too young at the time to realize what was happening all around. Besides, the fallout from Operation Tiger was still casting a shadow on my life,' Mattie said, picking up a photograph of Clara.

'If you two will excuse me,' Katie said. 'I need to get ready to meet Patrick.'

Ten minutes later when she went to say goodbye, Katie heard Noah asking if Mattie would give him a tour of the evacuation area sometime.

'Yes, of course,' Mattie said. 'Maybe when my friend Henri arrives. I know he'd enjoy it – and you know more about the history of World War Two down here than I do, despite growing up here. You off?' she asked, turning to look at Katie. 'Don't let him bully you, Katie. I have a feeling that Patrick will use any means he can to get his own way. Do what *you* want.'

'I intend to. See you later,' Katie said.

EIGHTEEN

Katie made her way through town to A Good Yarn. It was the only place she could think of that would guarantee her some privacy for half an hour to think about things. She pulled out her phone to ring Lara and ask her advice. Her finger hovered over the speed-dial button before she sighed and closed the phone down. Lara didn't like Patrick so her advice was bound to be biased. This was something she had to decide for herself.

Carefully locking the door behind her, Katie stood for a few moments looking around the shop she'd worked so hard on. With its shelves full of wool, souvenirs, craft kits and various other bits and pieces she knew it was a welcoming and pleasant place for customers. Sales had improved in the weeks she'd been open and now that the summer season was getting underway she was hopeful she'd get even busier. As she moved around the shop she made a mental note to order some more of the lightweight lacy wool; there were only three balls left. The postcard rack needed filling too.

In the clubroom, she automatically plumped up the cushions on the chairs, checked coffee supplies and straightened the pile of audio tapes on the table by the sewing machine.

The club was fitting well into the business, with the members gearing up to help her make a success of World-wide Knit in Public Day just a few weeks away.

Only last week they'd decided to have a sponsored knitting marathon on the day. Plans were also being made for a Christmas craft bazaar. Would Mattie be prepared to take on the organization if she returned to Bristol?

Katie climbed up to the attic room. She glanced into the bedroom as she went past. Her new mattress had arrived yesterday and she'd happily made up the bed. Now everything was ready for her to move in. Despite Leo's reservations. Leo. Katie pushed all thoughts of Leo firmly from her mind.

If Patrick hadn't arrived unexpectedly she'd planned to move in by this weekend but his arrival had complicated things. It had seemed easier to stay at the cottage but she'd definitely decided to move in this week and give Mattie back her space.

Opening the window, she took a deep breath as she looked out over the river towards the castle. Did she really want to leave again? Let people down? More importantly, let Mattie down? Why hadn't her dream job materialized before? Why hadn't Patrick proposed before? A little niggle in her head responded with, 'Because he didn't need to'. Round and round went her thoughts until finally she closed the window and left to meet Patrick.

Patrick was sitting in his car on the embankment by the Royal Avenue Gardens waiting for her and leant across to kiss her cheek as she slid into the passenger seat. The diamond solitaire engagement ring in its opened box sparkled in the sunshine on the dashboard.

'I was afraid you were going to be late,' he said, 'and I really do need to leave on the next ferry but one. So, Katie....' He turned to look at her. 'Are you staying down here or coming back to me and your proper career?'

'Can I have some more time to think about it, please, Patrick? Get the summer season over. See how....'

Patrick shook his head and interrupted her. 'Sorry, no. Today is decision time. If you're not joining me in the company I need to find someone else to take your place to start organizing things.'

The niggling feeling she'd had suddenly fell into place inside her head as Katie realized what was happening. Patrick was putting his new company before their own engagement and personal happiness.

Silently, Katie stared out of the window and knew there was only one answer she could give Patrick. She sat there trying to put her decision into words that wouldn't be too hurtful for him.

He reached out and took her hand in his. 'I have missed you, Katie. Please come back to me. Accept my ring.'

Katie turned to look at him. 'You say you've missed me. That you want to marry me – but do you love me, Patrick? You haven't hugged me really close since you arrived – and you've never uttered those three little words.'

'Katie, I've told you before, I'm not a demonstrative type of man. I do want you in my life so if it helps you to decide – I love you.'

Katie smiled faintly. 'You sound like a certain prince

wondering what that thing called love was.' She took a deep breath before adding, 'You've been a good friend and a good boss but I don't think you love me. I'm a convenient and useful solution to certain things current in your life. In other words, I think you're just trying to use me for your own ends.'

As he went to protest, Katie continued, 'Just listen. You think I'm wasting my time down here, that I'm only doing it for Mattie. The truth is, I love running A Good Yarn. I also love living back down here. A year ago if you'd offered me my dream job in the media I'd have been there, no question. But today....' Katie shook her head. 'Today it's not what I want any more. I guess I've outgrown those dreams because now my dream is to make a success of A Good Yarn. So I'm staying down here. It's where my life is now.'

Silently she stared out at the boats on the river and watched a seagull land on the roof of a boat-trip kiosk before turning to Patrick and saying gently, 'I don't want to marry you either, Patrick. I've realized I don't love you any more than you love me. I can't marry you without loving you.' She removed her hand from his. 'I'm sorry, your ring is not for me.' Leaning forward she closed the lid on the ring box.

'Your decision,' Patrick said, picking up the ring box and putting it in the glove compartment. 'Have to say I think it's the wrong one but then I would, wouldn't I? Can't believe you're turning not only me down but also the final chance of having any sort of media-based career. Think the regrets will begin to haunt you in about a year. You'd better go.'

Katie opened the car door, turned to give Patrick a gentle goodbye kiss on the cheek and got out.

Before she closed the car door she leant in and looked at Patrick sadly. 'I'm truly sorry, Patrick. I wish you all the luck in the world with your business. I also hope you meet somebody and fall in love.' She smiled at him briefly before adding, 'Go and get in the ferry queue. Safe journey back to Bristol for your meeting.' She closed the car door before turning and walking swiftly away.

Praying that Patrick would make for the Higher Ferry and not drive past her along the one-way system to take the Lower Ferry, Katie hurried along the embankment before turning up into Hawley Road and making for the steps in Fairfax Place that led up to Higher Street. Once she knew there was no danger of Patrick driving past and – and what? Begging her to change her mind? She slowed down to a normal walking pace and thought about what she had said to him.

It was true, her dreams had changed since she'd taken over A Good Yarn and she was happy she'd taken the decision to return. But, and there was always a but, Katie thought wryly, would she have cause to regret turning Patrick's offers down in the future? What if she failed with the business and Mattie had to close it down anyway? What if there were more break-ins? Damage to the stock hadn't been too bad this last time but what if it happened again? Mentally, Katie shook herself. The burglar alarm was fitted and it was only a matter of days now before she moved into the flat.

A Good Yarn wasn't going to fail. Business was already picking up both with locals and the ever-growing number of tourists. Mattie had already said this summer season was showing signs of being the best for several years. With that happy thought Katie set off in the direction of home to tell Mattie that Patrick had no part to play in her future.

Noah had left when Katie let herself into the cottage and Mattie was busy clearing things away. She looked up as Katie walked into the kitchen.

'Well? What's happening?'

'Patrick's on his way back to Bristol – without either a new production manager or a fiancée.'

The look of sheer relief that flitted across Mattie's face as she realized Katie had turned Patrick down on both counts was something Katie knew she would always remember.

'I'm so pleased,' Mattie said. 'You're making such a success of A Good Yarn, I know you won't regret it.' Mattie wiped a tear away. 'I was so afraid you were going to turn away from everything – and everyone – down here.'

Katie hugged her hard. 'I would never turn away from you, Mattie,' she said.

'You're moving into the flat, though,' Mattie said. 'Can't persuade you to change your mind about that?'

Katie shook her head. 'Sorry. You've got Henri's visit to look forward to, so you won't be alone for long. Wouldn't want to be in the way when he arrives.'

'You wouldn't be in the way.' Mattie squirted washing-up liquid into the bowl. 'Might be better if you were around,' she muttered.

'What are you worrying about? Henri sounds like a real gentleman. You said you were great mates on board the boat.'

'We were – that's the problem. My cottage is a world away

from all that luxury. What if he takes one look at it and finds it all beneath him?'

'He won't. Nobody in the real world lives permanently in the luxury you described on the boat.'

'I think Henri might,' Mattie said quietly. 'I did try to tell him I could only afford the suite because of a cancellation, but he shrugged it off. Said something about money not being the be-all of life. In my experience people only say things like that when they've got lots.'

NINETEEN

Katie placed her salad supper on the tray, poured a glass of rosé and carried everything upstairs. Sitting in the wicker chair, her supper on the coffee table in front of her, she opened her mobile and pressed Lara's number.

'Hi. I'm about to eat my supper in the flat for the first time.'

'Great. How does Mattie feel about you moving in?'

'Right now she's getting the cottage ready for this Henri she met on the cruise. It was one of the reasons I wanted to move now – not only to give them space but also so she wouldn't be alone. Can you come down this weekend?'

'Flat-warming party?'

'Yes.'

'Will Patrick be at this party?'

'No. It's over,' Katie said, as she filled Lara in with what had happened between her and Patrick. 'I would have leapt at the job a year ago, though,' Katie added.

'I'm rather more relieved you didn't accept his ring, to be honest,' Lara said. 'Thank God you've come to your senses at last and given the tosser his marching orders.' Lara's relief was clear down the phone.

Katie sighed. 'I know he was never your favourite person but he wasn't totally bad. We did have fun together. So, are you coming to my flat-warming party or not?'

'Of course. Daisy will be thrilled to have another sleep-over at her cousins. Want any help with food?'

'Only planning to have nibbles – and lots of champagne!'

'We'll bring a bottle and some kettle crisps for Leo. He is coming, I presume?'

'Haven't seen him to invite him yet. I expect he'll turn up, especially when he knows Dexter is coming.'

Putting the phone down after her call, though, Katie wondered about Leo. Patrick's arrival with his job offer and proposal had certainly thrown her into a quandary for a few days but Leo's reaction had been unexpected to say the least. As for those moments of intimacy and the kisses they'd shared before Patrick interrupted them, had they meant anything to him? Perhaps he was regretting them and was keeping his distance from embarrassment? Katie shook her head. She'd never known Leo to be embarrassed. There had to be another reason.

It was good the next day to only have to go downstairs for the weekly evening meeting of the club. Katie, looking around as the meeting was getting underway, marvelled again at the way the club had taken off. Membership had increased over the last few weeks, as had the diversity of the crafts. Mattie – in the far corner, explaining the intricacies of an Aran pattern to one of the regulars – glanced across and smiled.

Thanks goodness they were back to being friends again.

Whether Mattie had told Leo about her turning Patrick down, Katie didn't know. He'd certainly not rushed to get in touch if Mattie had told him, Katie thought as she prepared to hand out the publicity leaflets she'd printed for World-wide Knit in Public Day.

Irritating as he was she did miss having him boss her around. She'd ring him tomorrow. Invite him to the party. She knew Lara would have words with her if Leo wasn't there.

Behind her she heard Trisha squeal as Emma Pine arrived, showing off a new three-cluster engagement ring. 'Wow. That's some ring,' Trisha said.

'Congratulations, Emma,' Katie said. 'When's the wedding?'

'Oh, not for ages yet,' Emma said. 'Tristan fancies a Christmas wedding after his next tour of duty.'

'Tristan?'

'He's in the navy,' Emma explained.

As people crowded around Emma to see the ring and offer their congratulations, Katie stepped back and busied herself with the coffee machine. Emma was going to be a sailor's wife and not a farmer's. Not Leo's, as she'd initially thought when Emma had walked in.

'Well, that's a cause for celebration,' Mattie said.

'Wonder if Leo knows – and how he feels about it,' Katie said. 'They're quite close, aren't they?'

'Oh, he'll be pleased for her. They never were more than friends. He's known for months she'd met someone special,' Mattie said.

Trisha joined them just then. 'Can I have two coffees, please, for Emma and me? Isn't it exciting about her and

Tristan. I've got some news too.' She spooned some sugar into one of the cups before adding, 'I've got a date with Noah Jnr tomorrow night.'

'What about Gary?' Katie asked. 'You be careful. If he finds out he could turn nasty.'

'Nothing to do with him. We've broken up. My mum is over the moon about it. Says he wasn't good enough for me – even if he does have a sir way back in his family. She can't believe I'm going out with Noah. She thinks he's the biz.'

'Glad to hear it, Trisha – but Katie's right. Be careful. Gary and his family have a habit of harbouring grudges. You won't go disappearing off to America, will you?' Mattie said.

'Fat chance of that happening. I've still got three years at college to look forward to.'

'You finished for the summer now?' Katie asked. 'I could do with some more help in the shop on weekdays – starting this week when Mattie is going to be busy with her ship-board Romeo.'

'Don't be silly,' Mattie said. 'Henri's just a new friend I'm looking forward to meeting again.'

'He obviously can't wait to see you again as he's brought the date forward,' Katie teased. 'You sure there wasn't even a slight on-board romance you've not told us about?'

'Now you are being silly. We're both too old for that kind of nonsense. Are we going to listen to a tape tonight or not? Soon be time to pack up.'

Katie smiled. 'It's in the machine all ready to go. Final chapter of Katie Fforde's *Wedding Season*. I'll go and press the button.'

*

Mattie smoothed the quilt cover down for a final time and hoped that Henri would find the room comfortable. Years ago it had been Clara's room but the only thing that remained from that time was the small rag rug – which sat in front of the chest of drawers beside the window – they'd spent one winter making together.

Crossing to the window Mattie stood for several moments looking out at the river. It was a long time since she'd had anybody to stay – apart from Katie, of course, but she was different. She'd heard about how holiday friendships had failed to live up to their promise once people were back in the real world.

Her friendship with Henri had flourished in the relaxed cosmopolitan atmosphere of the cruise ship. Would Henri find the day-to-day routine of her ordinary life – and by implication her – dull by comparison? How would he like this part of the world? Would he enjoy the excursions she planned for them to take? Would they have anything to say to each other away from the detached world of life on board ship?

Mattie shook her head. Too late for silly worries like this. Henri would be here soon. She needed to get lunch ready.

When Henri arrived an hour later, she found she'd been worrying unnecessarily. From the moment he stepped out of his taxi they slipped back into the easy friendship that had developed between them on holiday.

'I was expecting Bert to bound out and meet me,' Henri said as Mattie led him into the cottage.

'He's down at A Good Yarn,' Mattie explained. 'I wasn't sure how you were with dogs?'

'Adore them. Have promised myself once I'm settled again, getting a dog is at the top of my list.'

'We'll walk down later and fetch him. I'll show you around the town at the same time. Incidentally we've been invited to Katie's flat-warming this evening. If you're not too tired after your journey?'

Henri shook his head. 'Sounds fun. I hope Katie didn't move out because I was visiting?'

Mattie shrugged. 'Maybe influenced things a little. She's always said she was going to live above the shop and the break-in spurred her on to getting the place ready. I think she's pleased your visit has given her the excuse to move.' Mattie smiled at Henri. 'She says she's giving us space.'

TWENTY

'Room in the fridge for this?' Lara asked, handing Katie a bottle of champagne. 'Are we the first here?'

'Always room for champagne,' Katie said, taking a cold bottle out and replacing it with the new one. 'Go on up. Mattie's up there waiting to introduce you to Henri.'

'Leo coming?' Dexter asked. 'I wanted to talk to him.'

'He'll be here later,' Katie said. 'I think.'

Lara glanced at her. 'You two still not talking?'

Katie shrugged. 'Apparently not.' She led the way upstairs.

'Wow. You've done an amazing job,' Lara said. 'I love it.' She moved across to look at the sailing picture Katie had hung on the wall between the two windows. 'Nice. Oh, damn. I've left your flat-warming pressie in the car.'

Dexter looked at Lara and shook his head. 'I'll go and get it. Don't eat all the food while I'm gone.'

'I'll come down and let you out,' Katie said. 'Once everyone is here I'll need to lock the shop door. You can take a key with you, OK?'

Katie was pleased to see both the Noahs as Dexter strolled off along Lower Street.

'Vicky not back yet?' she asked.

'Waiting for a flight change. My mother has finally agreed to come for a holiday,' Noah Snr said. 'Should arrive sometime next week, fingers crossed.'

Trisha and Emma were the next to arrive. Katie locked the door and followed them upstairs.

Lara and Henri, who'd apparently been a keen sailor in his youth, were talking boats.

'I'm looking forward to a trip on the river next week,' Henri said. 'Not sailing, though, unfortunately.'

'If you fancy a sail, get Mattie to take you up to my brother's boatyard,' Lara said. 'He'll lend you a boat – might even crew for you if you're lucky.'

'*Merci* Lara, not sure time will allow, this visit,' Henri said, looking across at Mattie. 'But next time it would be a treat.'

Katie was pouring a glass of champagne when Lara sidled up to her. 'So what gives with you and Leo?'

Katie shrugged. 'You tell me. Haven't seen him in ages. I didn't even speak to him when I rang to invite him this evening, just left a voice message asking him to let me know. I haven't heard a word. Top-up?' she asked, holding the bottle out to Lara and pouring when she nodded.

Lara frowned. 'Not like Leo to sulk. You must have really upset him.'

'Oh, sure. It's bound to be my fault,' Katie said.

'If he doesn't come this evening, I'll ring him in the morning,' Lara said. 'Sort it out.'

'Don't you dare.' Honestly, Lara could be so bossy and interfering sometimes. 'I'm quite capable of talking to Leo and finding out just what is bugging him.'

Katie was handing blinis topped with local crabmeat around when she heard the shop door slam. Dexter was back. A minute later he appeared holding a party gift bag – and followed by Leo.

'Hope you like this,' Dexter said, handing Katie the bag.

'Thank you,' Katie said. 'Hi, Leo. I'll get you both a drink.' She moved across to the table. Leo had come after all. Shame he hadn't bothered to change out of his usual jeans and sweatshirt, though.

Once everyone had food and a drink, Katie opened her present from Lara and Dexter. A Simon Drew rabbit print that had Katie laughing out loud. 'Oh, that's brilliant. I know just where I'll put it. Thank you.' Hoping Leo would offer to hang it for her she glanced across at him but he didn't say anything.

'Mattie and I haven't seen you recently,' Katie said. Better to include Mattie rather than admit she'd missed having him around.

'Been busy. Silage-making time,' Leo said.

'Not avoiding us, then?'

Leo sipped his champagne and didn't answer.

Katie, taking his silence to mean yes, bit her lip before saying quietly, 'If you haven't heard, I turned both Patrick's offers down.'

Leo turned to look at her.

Katie shrugged. 'Just wanted you to know. Not that it appears you're interested.'

Leo stared at her. 'I'm glad you said no to Patrick. But is living down here always going to be enough for you, Tiggy?' Leo asked. He put his glass down and gently kissed her on the cheek before she realized his intention. 'Sorry I can't stay. Got a sick sheep back at the farm.' He raised his hand in farewell. 'Sorry, folks, got to go. Mattie, Henri, I'll see you.' With that, he was gone.

Katie sighed. Sick sheep explained his clothes but not his offhand attitude with her. Getting their friendship back on track was clearly going to be difficult.

Sitting chatting over a leisurely lunch out on the terrace on the Monday after the party, Mattie told Henri about the planned drive around the area with Noah Snr. 'It's been arranged for later today. You will join us? We could always go on our own another day if you prefer.'

'I'm fine,' Henri said. 'I've been reading up on Operations Overlord and Tiger so am interested to see the actual places. Going with someone who knows their history will make it special too.'

'Noah Snr is a lot more knowledgeable about it all than I am,' Mattie said. 'Which makes me feel rather ashamed as it's part of my history. But then, I have rather avoided learning about certain issues in my life.'

'I'm sure you know more than you realize. It's amazing the amount of information one unconsciously absorbs as a child and then forgets.' Henri glanced at her. 'It's also possible you have deliberately blocked the memories of that particular aspect of your childhood.'

Mattie nodded. 'I'm sure there's a certain amount of truth in what you say, but Noah has done a serious amount of research for his documentary.' She stood up. 'I'll clear these things and then we'll walk down into town.'

Noah Snr was waiting for them in the shop when they arrived and apologized for being alone.

'Noah Jnr has gone up to Bristol to collect Vicky and my mother,' he said. 'They finally got a flight out.'

Mattie turned to Katie. 'Are you joining us for the trip out to Torcross?'

'No can do I'm afraid. Stuff to do down here.'

'Can I leave Bert with you then?'

'Of course,' Katie said. 'I'll take him for a walk when I close and then pop him back to the cottage. Shall I organize some supper for later – or will you be eating out?'

'I was planning to introduce Henri and Noah to the delights of fish and chips at the pub,' Mattie said. 'So don't worry about us.'

TWENTY-ONE

Henri looked around him appreciatively as Noah Snr negotiated the narrow twisting road out through Stoke Fleming, past Blackpool Sands, up the steep hill into Strete and then finally dropped down and round the last bend onto the long coastal road that led to Torcross.

'It's certainly a beautiful part of the world. Is that obelisk significant?' Henri asked, looking at a large granite stone erected on the seaward side of the road as they drove past.

'Sure is. Shall we take a closer look?' Noah said, pulling into the nearby car park. 'It was a gift from the United States.'

Standing in front of the obelisk and reading the dedication to the people of the South Hams from a grateful US Army, Henri shook his head. 'Operation Overlord must have come as a terrible shock to the people in the villages.'

Noah nodded. 'It was a sacrifice they had no say in, which made it harder, I imagine. For the common good at a time of war. But six weeks isn't long to literally pack up everything – from the smallest chick to the largest bull – and leave your home to face who knew what.'

'All because the coastline and beaches resemble those in

Normandy where the invasion of France was to happen?' Henri asked.

'The exercises they were able to practise here were invaluable for the actual D-Day landings,' Noah said.

'It's all so normal now. As if nothing ever disturbed the peace and beauty of this place – no visible scars. Just the obelisk to remind,' Henri said.

'Every now and again we get unexploded bombs turning up, especially after a storm,' Mattie said. 'Sometimes it causes a mini-evacuation along the coast road. Haven't had a scare for a few years, though.'

'Ready to move on to Torcross now?' Noah asked. 'I want to show you the tank and tell you something about Operation Tiger.'

Mattie gave a mock groan. 'What is it with you men? Anything mechanical connected to the war and you're fascinated.'

'Mattie, this tank was under the sea for about forty years,' Noah said. 'Amazingly, the tracks still moved when it was pulled out onto the road.'

There was the usual crowd of tourists surrounding the tank when Noah pulled into the car park a few minutes later.

'I'll leave you to tell Henri all about it. I'll go across to the restaurant and organize a table for supper,' Mattie said. Supper conversation tonight would, of course, revolve around the war and that tank. Was she ready to join in with her childhood memories of that dreadful time? Speaking about it would at least show Henri she was trying to keep her promise to him to put past events into perspective. A glass of wine before they joined her would help.

Half an hour later when the two men sat at the window table she'd managed to reserve, the bottle of red she'd ordered was half empty. Henri, holding a book, glanced at her.

'Are you OK? Tonight is difficult for you?'

Mattie smiled. 'I'm fine. What have you got there?'

Henri handed her the book. *The Forgotten Dead* by Ken Small and Mark Rogerson.'

'Have you read it?' Noah asked.

Mattie shook her head. 'No.' Looking at Henri she said, 'When you've read it you'll have to tell me what it says about Operation Tiger.'

'I'll lend you the book. You can read it for yourself,' Henri said.

'I know Operation Tiger changed the direction of my life,' Mattie said. 'I became my mother's only daughter. A daughter she expected to do the things Clara was supposed to do. Of course I could never take her place in my mother's affections, a fact which was spelt out to me for the rest of her life. "If only Clara had lived" was my mother's constant refrain in my ears.'

Mattie poured herself another glass of wine from the carafe on the table.

'Clara's birthday was April 18th and Hal had managed to get a couple of hours leave and they spent the evening together. Clara was so happy when she came home. She waltzed into my room and whispered to me that after the war was over Hal wanted her to go to America and live with him there – and she was going to marry him whatever our parents said.' The wine in Mattie's glass slopped over the edge as she twirled it round. Gently Henri took it from her and placed it on the table before taking hold of her hand.

'A few days later,' she continued, 'there were these rumours circulating about E-boats torpedoing several tank landing craft out in Start Bay killing hundreds of American servicemen – and no word from Hal to say he was OK. Clara was beside herself. It was his best friend who finally came to find her and tell her Hal had definitely been on one of the tank landing craft that had been torpedoed.'

Mattie fell silent, gazing out of the window at the sea where the tragedy had happened all those years ago. She bit her lip, remembering the awful scream that had rung throughout the house as the young officer, who had only narrowly escaped death himself in the incident, broke the terrible news to Clara.

Henri squeezed Mattie's hand tightly.

'Clara sank into a decline that day,' Mattie finally continued. 'My parents said she'd had a breakdown and packed her off to stay with cousins for a month in Penzance to get over it.'

'When she came back, how was she?' Henri asked.

'Different. Morose. My lovely big sister had changed out of all recognition.' Mattie reached for her glass and took a sip.

'On June 5th as we were all watching the harbour emptying she upped and left. I never saw her again. For months I kept hoping she'd come home and then the accident happened.' Mattie pressed her knuckles against her lips in a forlorn attempt to keep the tears at bay.

Silently Henri handed her a handkerchief and Mattie

smiled her thanks. 'I've spent all my life wishing Operation Tiger had never taken place. It's only now I'm realizing how big a tragedy it really was – not only for me but also the Americans.'

TWENTY-TWO

'Come on then, Bert old boy. We'll walk out to the castle and then take you home to the cottage,' Katie said, locking the shop door behind her.

It was a lovely evening and Katie strolled along thinking about her decision to give up all ideas of a career in the media and concentrate on A Good Yarn. She had so many ideas for the shop now she knew for certain where her future lay.

Having her own space again was great. And Mattie surely appreciated the cottage being her own especially now Henri had arrived. Living above the shop would hopefully be more of a deterrent to burglars than any burglar alarm, despite Leo and his misgivings about her moving in. Ah, Leo.

Still no word from him since his brief appearance at the party. She needed to talk to him if only to clear up any misconceptions he still held. She wanted him to know returning to live here was the best decision of her life and she had no intention of leaving again.

Dodging around the holidaymakers still loitering on the paths near the castle and its grounds, Katie impulsively carried on round the steep bend that lead to the Compass Cove footpath. She'd go and see him right now. If he wasn't home it would be a wasted journey but at least Bert would have had a good walk.

Shortening Bert's lead to keep him closer to heel, she ignored the lower coastal path and took the narrow lane that wound its way up past the old coastguard cottages. Leaving the breathtaking view to her left, she began to make her way along the inland coastal path.

Twenty minutes later, Katie – walking down Castle Farm track – was relieved to see lights on in the kitchen. Leo came out of the farmhouse when Meg began to bark her welcome.

'Hi,' Katie said.

'Bert looks like he could do with some water,' Leo said, pointing to the small trough he kept filled with water for Meg at the side of the door.

Katie slipped Bert's lead off. 'Could I have a glass too, please?'

Silently, Leo ushered her into the kitchen and poured her a glass of water.

'Thanks. Why did you run out on me at the party?' she asked quietly, looking at him.

'I told you. Sick sheep. I wasn't in the mood for partying.'

Katie drank her water, willing Leo to say something more. Ask her how she was. Jeez, why didn't he say something, anything, rather than just stare at her? She put the glass down on the working surface.

'OK. Thanks for that. I'd better be getting back to the flat. Lots to do. Can't quite believe I've been living there for nearly a week. No sign of a break-in yet. So that's got to be a result.' Ha. Leo's lips twitched as if he was trying not to smile at that.

'I've got one of my famous lasagnes in the Aga,' he said. 'Stay for supper?'

The unexpected invitation took Katie by surprise and she hesitated – torn between the two of them having a proper talk and wanting to get home to the flat. Besides, the shop accounts were also crying out for her attention.

'I can probably find some raspberries and clotted cream for dessert,' Leo added. 'If that helps you decide.'

'Mmm,' Katie laughed. 'You sure know how to persuade me. OK. But I mustn't stay too long. I want to get at least an hour's work in on the accounts this evening.'

'How's Mattie? Henri? How's he with Mattie?' Leo placed a chopping board and a knife on the work surface.

'Very attentive,' Katie said. 'They complement each other well,' she added. 'Mattie and Noah have taken him out to Slapton and Torcross as he's interested in the World War Two history of the area.'

Leo moved across to the fridge. 'Wine?'

'Please,' Katie said, nodding.

Sipping her wine by the Aga with Bert settled at her feet Katie looked around the kitchen appreciatively, while Leo, having refused her offer of help, prepared a salad.

'I love what you've done to this kitchen. It's how I always imagine a farmhouse kitchen should be.' She kept the thought, 'It's a real family kitchen,' to herself.

'Thanks. How's business at the shop?'

'Fine. Trying to organize the publicity for the Worldwide Knit in Public Day at the moment. The club are having a knitting marathon in Avenue Gardens.' Katie sighed. 'It's going to be a busy week. Could do without it being so close to the D-Day anniversary celebrations but nothing I can do about that.' She took a sip of her wine. 'Mattie was talking about the commemorative river trip on the sixth. Are you coming to that?'

'Of course. Dad always insists we join in. Don't remember Mattie ever joining that before, though. She must definitely be coming to terms with things.' Picking an onion out of the veg basket, Leo glanced at her.

'Katie, about the other day,' he said, expertly peeling and cutting the onion ready to toss it into the salad bowl.

'You want to apologize for calling me stupid? And for storming off for no reason? Not to mention being a party pooper?'

'No, I certainly don't. I was so angry with you that Sunday when you were meeting Patrick; I didn't dare stay in the same room.' He picked up a tomato and sliced it into quarters. 'I don't want to apologize about anything. I just want to talk to you about the evening in the shop when you fell of the ladder. And about how I feel.'

'Oh, that evening,' Katie said, smiling at the memory.

'Yes. Before Patrick arrived and interrupted things.' Leo picked up another tomato and concentrated on slicing it into quarters for several seconds before giving her a serious look.

'Katie, I just want to know,' he began. At the same moment, an urgent 'beep beep' began to emit from a pager on the work surface.

'Damn! Fire shout. Gotta go. Stay and eat something. If you leave before I get back, lock up and take the key with you. I've got a spare. Bye.'

As he spoke Leo shrugged himself into his jacket, grabbed the pager, took his motorbike keys off the rack and ran out of the door.

Katie, standing in the farmhouse doorway, watched him roar down the farm track as if his life – or someone else's – depended on it. She sniffed the air. Already there was a pungent smell of smoke drifting up from town.

'Be careful, Leo,' she called out to his disappearing back. Just what was he about to encounter in town?

Back in the kitchen, she finished preparing the salad and placed it in the fridge before washing the utensils and wiping the work surface down. Carefully she lifted the lasagne out of the Aga and checked it before placing it in the slow oven. There was no way she could eat anything without Leo. She glanced out of the window. Should she wait for Leo to return or go – walk down Weeke Hill and the long descent into South Town?

Walking alone in the countryside in the dark, even with Bert at her side, wasn't something that appealed. Moving across to close the kitchen window and draw the curtains, she heard the siren of a fire engine in the distance. Had she left anything on in the flat? Iron? Hairdryer? No both those items had been disconnected – in the case of the iron, for many days.

The noise of the siren decided for her and she settled anxiously into the chair at the side of the Aga to await Leo's return. She couldn't leave the farm until she knew he was home safe. And there was still that unfinished conversation – she needed to know what Leo had been about to say to her.

Finding the remote control for the small TV Leo had

placed on one of the dresser shelves, Katie started to flick through the channels before remembering Mattie didn't know where she was.

Pressing Mattie's home number on the mobile, she listened to the ringing tone. Perhaps Mattie and Henri weren't back from Slapton yet. She was about to switch off when a breathless Mattie answered.

'Katie, where are you? Is Bert with you?'

'Yes, Bert's with me up at Leo's place. Any idea where this fire is? Is it a bad one?'

'We haven't been back from Slapton long so no idea at the moment. There's lots of smoke down here and various roads are closed. Shouldn't think Leo will be back for a long time.'

'Oh,' Katie said, expelling a long breath.

'It's chaos down here. You're best off out of it staying up there,' Mattie said. 'We'll see you in the morning. Bye. Got to go – Henri is trying to tell me something.' The dial tone buzzed in Katie's ear as Mattie hung up.

The phrase 'You're best off out of it' and the way Mattie'd hung up so quickly, jarred with Katie. A sudden icy fear gripped her. Had Mattie deliberately avoided telling her exactly where the fire was raging?

It couldn't possibly be A Good Yarn on fire, could it?

If only she'd left earlier and braved the walk down to town. Now it was pitch black outside and the thought of walking down the country lane and Weeke Hill was truly scary, even with Bert at her side. But she had to know where the fire was. She couldn't just stay up here and wait.

Reaching for her coat and Bert's lead, Katie's hand brushed against the board where Leo kept all his house and farm keys. Of course! Her car was in the barn. How stupid of her not to remember. She'd drive down and see for herself what was going on.

Five minutes later and Katie was on her way to town. The closer she got, the stronger the smell of smoke became. Past Warfleet, round the bend, up the slight hill ready towards the turning into Above Town and Mattie's cottage, Katie saw great clouds of smoke billowing in the night sky above the river.

Flashing blue lights and a policeman barring her way forced her to slam the brakes on before she could take the left fork.

'Sorry, miss, town's closed on account of the fire,' the policeman told her as she wound the window down. 'I'm afraid you'll have to turn around.'

'But I live in Above Town.'

The policeman shook his head. 'No traffic and no people until the fire is definitely under control. You'll have to turn round,' he repeated.

'Where is the fire?' Katie asked, hoping against hope it would be at the far end of town. But the policeman confirmed her fears.

'Down by the Lower Ferry.'

'What? My shop is down there!'

'I'm sorry, miss, but I can't let you through.'

'Do you know exactly which building's burning?' Katie asked desperately.

The policeman shook his head. 'Sorry.'

Frustrated, Katie slumped back against her seat. There was nothing for it but to go back to Leo's and wait. She turned the car and began to make her way back to the farm.

Once back at the farm, Katie couldn't settle but if she was going to spend the night in the farmhouse she'd need to find somewhere to sleep.

Feeling guilty, like an uninvited guest, Katie made her way upstairs to explore Leo's home. She pushed open the first door she came to. Leo's bedroom. The neatly made bed – the only piece of furniture in the room – was placed facing the curtainless window overlooking the sea. An open door on the far right wall gave a glimpse of the black and white tiles in the en-suite bathroom.

The next room was empty. Had Leo furnished only one bedroom? Katie sincerely hoped that wasn't the case – she didn't fancy crashing out on Leo's bed. The next door she tried opened on to a book-lined study complete with desk and computer and file boxes of what Katie took to be the farms accounts. She moved into the room to take a closer look at a collage of photos above the desk.

Mainly before and after photos of the modernization Leo had done at the farm, there were also a couple of him and his brother Joshua larking around on the river and a family group taken on holiday somewhere.

Tucked into the collage frame at the bottom was another photo which surprised Katie with its presence but made her smile as she read the inscription scrawled across the bottom, before she turned and left the study.

She breathed a sigh of relief when she opened the door of the last room and discovered what was clearly a guest room with its pretty floral wallpaper and curtains and, importantly, a made-up bed. She would sleep in there tonight.

Back downstairs, she put the kettle on the Aga, found the

cafetière and spooned some coffee in. While she was waiting for the kettle to boil she took the lasagne out of the bottom oven. It would spoil if it spent any more time in there. Best to reheat it when Leo got home.

Restlessly she took her phone out of her bag. Phoning Lara would pass some time. But it went straight to voice message so she left it. Maybe Lara would see a missed call message anyway and phone her.

Sipping her drink and half-heartedly watching an episode of some costume drama, Katie wondered about the fire and how long it would be before Leo came home. At midnight, she finally gave up waiting and – leaving the lights on in the kitchen – went to bed.

Taking off her shoes and jeans, Katie slipped under the duvet and settled down with little hope of sleeping. But the rhythmic one, two, three light from the lighthouse at Start Point flashing across the window every ten seconds was strangely soothing and she was asleep within minutes.

Three hours later, Bert – sleeping at the foot of the bed – gave a low-throated warning growl that woke Katie with a start. Her head spun for a few seconds before she remembered where she was. Leo must finally be home. Quickly she reached for her jeans and pulled them on.

Downstairs Leo was leaning against the Aga, the strain of the last hours showing clearly on his face.

'You OK?' Katie asked.

'Been better but nothing a few hours' sleep won't sort out.' Leo flexed his shoulders tiredly.

'It was a bad fire, wasn't it?' Katie said.

'Big and bad enough, though not in the league of the one

that raged through the medieval buildings a few years ago, thank God. That was terrible. The whole town was in shock for weeks afterwards.'

'Is A Good Yarn still standing?' Katie asked in trepidation.

Leo glanced at her sharply. 'How do you know where the fire was?'

'I drove down. The police wouldn't let me through even though I told them who I was.'

'Whole area was cordoned off,' Leo said. 'Standard procedure.'

'Well, is it? Still standing?' Katie said.

Leo nodded. 'Yes. The fire started two buildings down from A Good Yarn,' He said quietly. 'We managed to get it under control before it reached the shop. The Old Salt House has suffered more. The top floor of A Good Yarn has suffered some minor fire damage but it could have been a lot worse. Good job you decided to walk up and stay here this evening.'

Katie stared at him. *Oh. My. God.* She could have been trapped in the flat by the fire.

Leo rubbed his eyes wearily.

'Can I get you anything? Tea? Coffee? Glass of wine? Heat up some lasagne for you?' Aware that she was babbling with relief, she said, 'I'm sorry. It's your house. Your kitchen. Not my place to offer.'

'Actually, Katie, all I really want is my bed,' Leo said.

'Of course,' Katie said quickly. 'I'm sorry. I'll see you at breakfast,' she added. 'Goodnight.' She turned to leave the kitchen.

'Goodnight. Katie?' Leo said, switching off the lights and preparing to follow her upstairs. 'Have to say I didn't expect to find you still here but thanks for staying.'

'Hope you don't mind.'

Leo shook his head. 'Course not. It's nice to come home to you,' and he smiled at her. 'Where are you sleeping?'

'The guest bedroom,' Katie said hurriedly. 'I didn't want to take your bed. I figured you were going to need it when you got back.'

As Leo looked at her intently, Katie cursed the flush that she could feel spreading across her face.

TWENTY-THREE

The smell of bacon woke Katie a few hours later. A quick splash of water on her face in the small en-suite shower room revived her but left her wishing for a toothbrush as she made her way downstairs.

'Morning. How do you like your eggs?' Leo asked.

'Umm, I'm really sorry but I don't eat breakfast,' Katie said. 'Just coffee will be fine and then I must go. Need to shower and change and get down to the shop. See for myself what the damage is.'

'At least have some toast with the coffee,' Leo said. 'I'll run you down to Mattie's and wait while you get ready and we'll go down to the shop together.'

'I'd be grateful for a lift back to town but you don't have to wait,' Katie said, helping herself to a coffee from the cafetière.

Leo shrugged. 'We'll see how you feel when we get to Mattie's.'

Katie put her coffee down on the table. 'Actually, can we forget coffee and breakfast please and just get down there now?'

Leo looked at her and sighed. 'OK. Let's go.'

Katie was silent as they drove down into town. What state was A Good Yarn going to be in? Leo's reassurances in the past had always played things down. His 'They've messed things up a bit' had failed totally to prepare her for what she found after the break-in. Was he doing the same with the 'minor' damage he'd mentioned last night?

Leo dropped her at Mattie's. 'I'll find somewhere to park and see you at the shop. OK? Don't worry. It's going to be all right.'

Mattie and Henri met her on the doorstep of the cottage.

'Ah good, you're back,' Mattie said. 'We're just going to walk down to the shop and see the damage in daylight. Bert can stay here.'

Despite the wind blowing in off the river, the air still smelled smoky as they walked down into Fairfax Place and along Lower Street. Apart from that acrid smell, everything seemed normal with people going about their daily business.

Leo joined them as they reached the ferry slipway. 'Katie, remember it's mainly superficial damage. I'm afraid the worse of it will be upstairs in the attic room. The shop itself should be relatively unscathed.'

Leo's reassurance did nothing to lessen Katie's shock at her first sighting of the fire-damaged buildings. The Old Salt House, the empty building next door but one to A Good Yarn, had clearly taken the brunt of the fire. Its stone facade was blackened, the top-floor windows had been blown out and there was a large hole in the roof by the chimney stack. Debris littered the cordoned-off pavement in front of it.

Although A Good Yarn had escaped major damage,

looking up at the blackened roofs Katie could see where the fire had reached.

'There was a bit of a north-easterly wind last night, which blew the sparks across,' Leo said, following her gaze. 'Luckily we managed to stop it spreading. There's some smoke damage up there, though.'

The lower floors appeared to be unscathed although the stone facade was blackened with soot and a wooden window-sill on the top floor appeared to be scorched.

'We know the fire started in the Old Salt House,' Leo said. 'Probably ancient wiring – although foul play hasn't been totally ruled out yet. Won't know for sure until the reports are in.'

'Those properties have been empty for ages, though,' Mattie said. 'Ever since the auction a couple of years ago when that development company bought both of them. Wanted A Good Yarn too but I didn't like the sound of them so I turned their offer down. Much to Ron's annoyance.'

'Lake and Bidder Property Developments?' Leo said.

'That's them,' Mattie said. 'Think they thought by adopting a couple of significant local names, everyone would warm to them.'

'Can we go in?' Katie said. 'See what it's like inside. Decide whether I can open up today – or whether I have to organize yet another major cleaning-up operation.'

She sighed. 'You know, sometimes I feel as though me and A Good Yarn are jinxed. This is the third time something has happened. Maybe you should sell it, Mattie.'

'Nonsense,' Mattie said briskly. 'No such thing as being jinxed. Things happen because they happen.'

'Or because somebody makes them,' Katie said quietly. 'Look who's over there in the pub doorway. Ron.'

As Mattie, Leo and Henri turned to look, Ron raised his hand and gave them a mock salute before walking quickly up the slope towards Newcomen Road and disappearing.

As Leo had promised, the shop itself was undamaged. It just needed a thorough airing to get rid of the smell, and the outside of the smoke-blackened windows to be cleaned. The apartment upstairs, though, was in a sorry state from smoke and water damage. Katie had a quick look and closed the connecting door. There was no way she could face it right now. It would have to wait until after Worldwide Knit in Public day.

Mattie and Leo were on their own when she got back downstairs. 'Where's Henri?'

'Gone off to have coffee with Noah Snr,' Mattie said. 'And then he's going back to the cottage to keep Bert company. How's the flat?'

'The damage could be worse but it's going to take some time to clean,' Katie said, sighing. 'Mattie, I hate to ask, but can I move back in for a few days?'

'You don't have to ask, you silly girl,' Mattie said. 'Of course you can.'

'I've got to get back to the farm. Expecting a delivery of grain,' Leo said. 'I'll try to come back down later to give you a hand.'

Mattie volunteered to stay on and man the till in case there were any customers, while Katie got to grips with airing everything and cleaning the windows.

Henri turned up with some sandwiches for lunch but left again soon afterwards.

'Don't you want to go to and keep him company?' Katie said.

Mattie shook her head. 'He's planning to work on his laptop for the afternoon. Making arrangements for when he leaves next week.'

Katie glanced across at her.

'You're really fond of Henri, aren't you?'

Mattie nodded. 'I'm going to miss him when he leaves, that's for sure.'

'He'll be back,' Katie said. 'He's told me he likes this area and plans to explore more of it – with you of course. You could always visit him in France.'

Mattie fiddled with the basket of knitted flowers on the counter. 'He wants me to go to Paris with him. Says everyone should go to Paris at least once in their lives.'

'Mattie, you must go. You've been tied to this place for so long, you deserve to enjoy yourself,' Katie said. 'To have a friend like Henri to show you his Paris – it'll be wonderful.'

Mattie sighed. 'I know you're right but....'

'But what?'

Mattie shook her head. 'I can't get used to the idea I'm free to do what I want to these days and ...' she hesitated.

Katie looked at her questioningly. 'And?'

'It's years since I've had a special friend like Henri,' Mattie said quietly. 'I can't help worrying I'll inadvertently spoil things by not being the kind of well-educated and travelled woman he's used to. I'm a bit of a country bumpkin really. Maybe he'll decide when he goes home the distance between us is too much.'

'Mattie, stop it!' Katie ordered. 'It's obvious that Henri

likes you just as you are. If you're meant to stay in touch when he leaves, you will. You're worrying unnecessarily about things that haven't happened.'

'I hope you're right,' Mattie said.

'You know I am. Now what?' Katie said as Mattie shook her head again.

'I'd forgotten about Bert. He'll be a problem if I go gallivanting off to Paris.'

'Bert is not a problem – and you know it,' Katie said laughing. 'He's as much at home down here these days as he is in your cottage. Right, the windows look OK. Are you all right staying for another half an hour? I could do with getting wool and stuff ready for Worldwide Knit in Public Day.'

Mattie looked at her watch. 'Need to leave in an hour. Leo's joining us for supper tonight and I want to do something special. You'll eat with us, won't you, now you're moving back in? You haven't got other plans?'

'No, no plans. I'll be there tonight,' Katie said. Maybe tonight would be the night she and Leo finally had their delayed talk.

TWENTY-FOUR

The evening before Worldwide Knit in Public Day all fourteen club members turned up to hear about the final preparations for the big day. Several of them had got sponsors and were hoping to raise some money for a local hospice and asked if they could put a charity collecting box on the stall.

'I'm hoping some of you will find different places around town to knit in,' Katie said. 'Coronation Park, the Boat Float, Bayards Cove, the library. Anywhere public where you can sit and knit!'

The following discussion over the best places to sit and knit was loud. 'I can't do it on my own,' one of them said. 'I'd feel silly sitting there knitting. People might stare. I need company.'

'I'll be in Avenue Gardens all day with table and chairs, and extra needles and wool in case people want to join in,' Katie said. 'So we'll make that HQ for the day. You can stay there or wander off to a seat by the Boat Float or wherever you feel happy. We just have to pray it doesn't rain. Now, has everyone got enough wool for a marathon knitting session?'

To Katie's relief, Worldwide Knit in Public Day dawned dry and sunny. Leo had volunteered to transport the table, chairs and wool supplies she needed to the Royal Avenue Gardens. By ten o'clock they were setting things up near the entrance arch under the interested gaze of passers-by.

'I can't stay this morning. Got some work to do up on the farm,' Leo said as they put the last chair in place. 'But I'll be back to do the return trip with this lot.'

'Thanks,' Katie said. 'Bye then,' and she watched him stride purposefully away. Supper at Mattie's the other evening had been fun. Both Mattie and Henri had been in top form but there hadn't been any opportunity to talk to Leo privately.

The shadow of the night Patrick had arrived was hanging over them like some sort of badly kept secret waiting to be brought out into the open, although there was less of an atmosphere between them now. When would Leo talk to her?

If only she could turn the clock back to before Patrick's arrival when everything between her and Leo had been normal. Well, apart from him kissing her, of course. That had never happened before.

Sighing, Katie turned back to the table and tried to concentrate on placing the wool, patterns and needles in what she hoped was an inviting display. Members of the club started to arrive and soon a small crowd had gathered out of curiosity, forcing everything else out of Katie's mind.

Mattie and Henri arrived at midday, by which time there were knitters throughout town and several in the gardens.

A party atmosphere was rapidly springing up – particularly when one of the club members turned up with some home-made nibbles and a bottle of wine.

Katie was about to leave and go down to A Good Yarn to check on Trisha when Noah Snr arrived with Vicky, Noah Jnr and an elegant older woman.

'Mattie, Katie, I'd like you to meet my mother, Elizabeth Emprey, and Mattie, this is my daughter, Vicky.'

'Pleased to meet you both,' Mattie said, shaking Elizabeth's hand and smiling. 'I'm sorry you've had such a sad time of things recently. Noah told us about his grand-mother dying and how you were having to cope with things. It's not easy, is it?'

Elizabeth shook her head. 'No. The most difficult part has been going through my mother's private papers.'

Vicky squeezed her grandmother's arm. 'But it's finished now, Grandma, and Great-grandma Kitty left us lots of exciting information about the family.' She turned to Mattie and Katie.

'There were some old family papers in a box that helped me with the research I was doing. I think Dad mentioned Anne Follett to you? She emigrated from here. Apparently she came from a large family who still have descendants living in the town.'

'How exciting,' Katie said. 'Do you have any names?'

'A few,' Vicky said. 'It's a bit complicated because the Follett branch of the family appears to have died out or merged into a family called Luttrell.'

'Leo and I have Luttrell relations,' Mattie said. 'What fun – we could turn out to be related!'

'But we're American, ma'am,' Noah Snr gently teased. 'Don't you have a problem with that?'

Mattie had the grace to look ashamed. 'No. That was a childish opinion I clung to for far too long. Besides, I like you and your family – and you can't help being American!'

'Perhaps you'd like to see some of the papers I've brought over with me,' Elizabeth said. 'You might even be able to help us in tracing the twentieth-century family line.'

'I'd love to see the papers and your family tree connections to the town,' Mattie said. 'Although I don't promise to be of much help.'

'Don't forget Great-uncle Nathaniel's letters,' Noah Jnr said. 'You did bring those with you?' he asked his mother anxiously. 'I haven't seen those yet.'

Elizabeth nodded. 'Yes, I brought them. And the photos.' She turned to Mattie. 'My 97-year-old mother left us one or two unexpected mementoes in her box of family papers. Secrets from her early life that we had no idea about.'

Mattie smiled in sympathy. 'It's difficult going through someone else's possessions, isn't it? Especially when it's too late for them to answer all the questions you want to ask. Look, why doesn't Noah bring you to the cottage for tea this afternoon?'

'Gee, I'm sorry, ma'am,' Noah Snr said. 'Mother and I already have an appointment this afternoon. Could we make it tomorrow?'

'Of course,' Mattie said. She turned to Katie. 'Now, anything I can do here? Otherwise Henri and I are going to sit by the Boat Float and knit.'

'You knit?' Katie said looking at Henri.

'*Oui*. Nothing fancy but I do like a new wool scarf every winter,' he said with a smile.

Katie watched them affectionately as they made their way across to a bench seat in the shade at the Boat Float. Mattie looked so right with her 'special' friend. There was soon an interested crowd gathered around them watching Henri knit.

Time passed quickly and at four o'clock a tired Katie was pleased to see Leo when he turned up, as promised, to help her take things back to A Good Yarn.

'Good day?' he said.

'Yes,' Katie nodded. 'The sponsored knitters have met their targets and people have been generous in donating to the charity box.'

Back at the shop, Trisha was happy too. 'I sold lots of wool and quite a few other things as well,' she said. 'Locals were asking about joining the club too. And people were so sympathetic about the fire.' Trisha looked at Katie.

'Great,' Katie said. Sensing there was something that Trisha wasn't telling her she said, 'Anything else?'

'Ron came in,' Trisha said. 'Said he wanted to offer you his sympathy over the fire.'

'Oh, he does, does he?' Katie said, remembering him slinking off, the morning after the fire.

'Wants you and Leo to go and see him,' Trisha said.

Surprised Katie looked at Leo, who shrugged.

'Did he say why?' Katie asked.

Trisha shook his head. 'No. Just said to tell you the sooner the better.'

'Well, I'm not running out there on Ron's say-so,' Katie said. 'We'll go tomorrow.'

'I can take you tonight,' Leo said. 'I'd quite like to hear what Ron has to say.'

Katie shook her head. 'Tomorrow will be fine. I really need to make a start on the apartment. I can't put it off any longer – the smoke and the smell up there is horrendous.'

'OK, tomorrow it is,' Leo said. 'I've got to get back to the farm for half an hour but I'll be back to give you a hand upstairs and then we'll have supper together. We still need to talk.'

'Supper sounds good,' Katie said, smiling. 'Shall I order a takeaway?'

'No. I'll organize something. See you in a bit,' Leo said, and left.

Back at the cottage, Mattie and Henri were sitting out on the terrace watching the boats on the river.

'I must say I'm looking forward to being out on the river and taking part in the D-Day Anniversary ceremony,' Henri said. 'Seeing the town from the river will be interesting too.'

'Let just hope the weather is kind to us,' Mattie said. 'Too much wind and choppy waves always make me feel seasick. Now, what shall we do for supper tonight?'

'Are Katie and Leo joining us?' Henri asked.

'No. I think Katie is going to do some work down at the shop. Not sure what Leo is up to. Hopefully helping Katie,' Mattie said. 'I've been waiting years for something to happen between those two and, everything crossed, I think it might be about to happen.'

'Been matchmaking, have you?' Henri teased.

Mattie shook her head. 'Those two are so completely right

for each other I don't understand why it's taken them so long to figure it out. Katie going away to be a journalist obviously didn't help but she's been back now for a couple of months. Leo should have told her how he feels by now – especially now that Patrick is out of her life. Previous boyfriend,' she added, seeing Henri's puzzled look.

'It's never that easy though, is it, telling someone how you feel, however old you are. Especially when you're not totally sure of their reaction.'

Mattie turned to look at him, surprised by the quiet intensity in his voice and waiting for him to say more. Instead he stood up and walked towards the garden wall before asking. 'Do you ever get tired of this view?'

Mattie shook her head. 'Never. There's always something happening on the river – if it's only watching the shadows of the clouds on the surface of the water as they pass across.' She went and stood beside him. 'Look, there are swans over there by Waterhead Creek. I wonder if they've made their usual nest down by the railway line.'

'I shall miss all this when I leave next week,' Henri said.

'You're definitely leaving next week?' Mattie said. 'I shall miss you.'

'Come with me,' Henri said. 'I've provisionally reserved a ticket for you,' he added quietly. 'We'll have a week in Paris for me to show you the sights like I promised and then we can go house-hunting on the Cote d'Azur. I've got until ten o'clock tonight to confirm my booking on the internet.'

'Oh, Henri,' Mattie sighed. 'A week in Paris sounds lovely but why do you need my help looking for a house?'

'Because you have to like what I buy. I'd hate to buy something only for you to see it and say you can't stay there with me because you don't like it.'

'I wouldn't do that, Henri,' Mattie said. 'I'm sure I'll like whatever you buy. It's just ...' she hesitated.

'What?'

'Meeting you on holiday, having you stay here – it's been wonderful. But life has to get back on track one day and our real lives are so far apart from each other, in all senses. You live in France and I live in Devon. Are we really going to be able to stay in close touch?'

'Definitely,' Henri said. 'The saying "It's a small world" has never been truer. As far as I'm concerned my "real life" now involves you, even if that means dividing our time between Devon and France. So, Mattie, can we see if our friendship will survive in "real life", as you put it?'

Mattie smiled tremulously. 'Oh, Henri, I don't know what to say.'

'Saying yes to Paris next week would be a good start.'

Mattie nodded. 'I'm definitely thinking about taking you up on that offer. So long as Katie doesn't mind having Bert for me again. Talking of Bert – he needs a walk before I start supper. Do you want to come with me?'

Henri shook his head. 'I think I'll go and confirm our tickets in case you change your mind.'

TWENTY-FIVE

Katie was upstairs at A Good Yarn when Leo returned that evening to collect her for their supper date.

'Have you talked to the insurance company yet about this?' he asked. 'They'll need to come and assess things.'

'Rang them this morning. They're sending someone beginning of next week. Oh, do you think I should leave everything as it is? Not even start to clean up a bit?'

'Might be a good idea,' Leo said, looking around. 'Otherwise you might risk not getting all the compensation you're entitled too.'

Katie sighed. 'I was so enjoying living up here too.'

'Mattie's pleased to have you back – even if it is for the wrong reason. I imagine she'll be grateful for the company too when Henri leaves.'

Katie laughed. 'I think it's me more likely to be missing Mattie if things pan out like I think they're going to.'

Leo looked at her, waiting for her to say more but she shook her head. It was not up to her to talk about Mattie's private life – even to Leo, her favourite nephew. Mattie would tell him – if he didn't guess the way things were going before.

'Right. If we're not going to make a start here let's go and have supper,' Leo said.

He waited while Katie locked up and made sure everything was secure before taking her by the hand. 'Come on. Car's up in Newcomen Road.'

'Where are we going for supper?'

'My place of course,' Leo said smiling. 'I'm not on call tonight so I promise not to run out on you.'

'Good,' Katie said, wondering if Leo would say what he wanted to talk about as they drove up to Castle Farm. But he pressed the button on the car's CD player and hits from the 80s filled the car as he drove.

Ten minutes later, Leo parked in front of the farmhouse. As she got out Katie asked, 'What do you want to talk to me about?'

'In a minute – let's get supper underway. Lamb chops and salad OK with you?'

'Sounds delicious,' Katie said, following him into the kitchen. 'Can I do anything?'

'I prepared everything earlier,' Leo said. 'So it's just a question of waiting for the chops to cook,' and he placed the prepared meat in the Aga before pouring them both a glass of wine.

'Santé,' Katie said, clinking her glass against Leo's. 'Can I ask you something?'

'Of course.'

'The night of the fire when I stayed here alone, I saw the photograph collage in the study.'

A smile crept across Leo's face. 'And?'

'That photo of you and me in Old Mill Creek taken when

I was about fifteen you've tucked into the frame ...' Katie
hesitated before continuing. 'Did you mean what you've
written across the bottom of it?'

Leo didn't answer directly, saying instead, 'Tiggy, you
remember the night you fell off the ladder in the shop and
Patrick arrived?'

'You mean the night you kissed me?' she asked quietly.
'The night you told me you didn't ever want to let me go?'

Leo nodded. 'Did it mean as much to you as it did to me?'

Katie nodded but before she could say anything Leo
continued.

'When you left to be a journalist I hoped you'd be back in
a couple of years, tired of city life and being a career girl. I
hated seeing you go but I knew I had to let you go without
telling you how I felt. You needed the freedom to meet other
people, have fun, to grow up away from home.' He took a sip
of his wine.

'Like you did at agricultural college,' Katie said.

Leo grinned at her. 'I couldn't wait to get back home but
I did enjoy those two years.'

'I bet you did,' Katie said, waiting to see where the
conversation was leading.

'You were too busy planning your escape from down here
and then building your career to notice me,' Leo said. 'But I
kept hoping that one day my Tiggy would return – but you
rarely visited and on the occasions you did, you seemed
content with your job, your life, your boyfriends. Then I
bought this place and farming being what it is, my life got
overtaken by work too. But I never stopped hoping you'd get
fed up with the rat race and come home permanently. The

words on that photo – Tiggy, the love of my life – were written from my heart years ago.' Leo fell silent for several seconds before saying, 'Tiggy, I just want to know how you feel about me.'

'That evening before Patrick arrived changed everything, Leo,' Katie said quietly. 'It was one of the main reasons I had to turn Patrick's offer down. I realized I liked my life back down here too much to give it up and....' She took a deep breath. 'I didn't want to leave you behind again.' She smiled at him. 'I even like you calling me Tiggy!'

Leo put his wine down and took her in his arms. 'Tiggy, you have no idea how happy that makes me.'

Katie lent forward and kissed him gently. 'Oh yes, I do.'

Leo groaned as he went to kiss her back, just as the strains of Old MacDonald began to emit from Katie's mobile.

'Ignore it. Let them leave a message. You can ring back later. Much later.'

'OK,' Katie murmured, nestling into his arms, only to go rigid with shock as the caller left a voice message.

'Katie, this is Henri. I need your help. Mattie is missing. I don't know what to do.'

Hearing Henri's words, Leo unwrapped his arms from around Katie and wordlessly moved to the Aga where he took the meat out, placing it on the work surface.

Grabbing his keys and coat he said, 'Come on, let's go. Ring Henri back – see if he has any ideas where she might be.'

Henri answered the phone immediately.

'Henri, we're on our way back,' Katie said. 'How long has Mattie been gone?'

'A couple of hours. Said she was taking Bert for his usual walk. I didn't accompany her because I needed to organize tickets. I think also she wanted some time alone.'

'Did she say which direction she was going?' Katie asked. What exactly had Mattie wanted time alone for?

'No. I didn't think to ask,' Henri said. 'She didn't take her mobile phone either. It's still here on the kitchen table.'

'We'll come down from Leo's farm via Weeke Hill,' Katie said, glancing at Leo who nodded in agreement. 'On the way we'll drive out to the castle and have a walk around out there. You stay at the cottage in case she turns up. Don't worry, Henri – knowing Mattie she's probably met someone and forgotten all about the time.'

Ending the call, Katie hoped that was the reason. Mattie being alone and in trouble didn't bear thinking about.

Leo drove slowly down Weeke Hill before turning right over the small bridge by Warfleet and making for Gallants Bower. There were still a few people enjoying an evening stroll, which Katie took to be a good sign.

'If Mattie was in trouble maybe someone has already found and helped her?' she said.

Leo shrugged. 'Maybe. It'll be dark soon. If we haven't found her by then we'll have to ring the hospital and contact the police. We'll park the car and go on foot when we get to the castle.' He indicated the glove box in front of Katie. 'There's a torch in there. We're going to need it.'

At the castle they searched and called. Walking slowly along, calling Mattie's name, the two of them listened for any response or the sound of Bert barking. Katie even looked in the graveyard surrounding St Petrox Church though she knew Mattie would never have taken Bert in there.

Katie quizzed everyone they passed. 'Have you seen a woman walking a big black dog?'

Everyone shook their heads. 'Sorry. No. We'll keep an eye out on our way back to town.' Katie, getting more and more frantic, had to be satisfied with their promises.

'Does she ever walk out to Sugary or Compass Cove?' Leo said.

'No. She does sometimes go as far as the Coastguard Cottages,' Katie said. 'We'd better have a quick walk up there.'

The two of them climbed the steep narrow path, winding its way up to the cottages, that Katie had walked with Bert herself only a few days ago. Tonight in the dusk, the steep drop on the left-hand side worried Katie. What if Mattie had gone over the edge? She shivered. Of course Mattie hadn't gone over the edge.

Leo noticed her looking at the way the cliff fell away from the path and protectively moved to her left without saying a word.

'Mattieee!' they both called at frequent intervals.

As they neared the top where the ground to the left levelled out, Leo suddenly stopped. 'Listen. I can hear a dog. Mattieeee!' he shouted. 'Mattieee! Bert!'

'Help! I'm over here,' a faint cry answered him.

Instantly Leo was off the pathway and sure-footedly making his way through the undergrowth towards the voice. Katie followed, her heart in her mouth, as she slipped and slithered her way behind Leo. A minute later and they'd found Mattie and Bert sheltering in the lee of some over-grown bramble bushes.

Leo dropped to his knees and knelt beside her. 'Thank God we've found you. Where do you hurt?'

'My ankle. Bert careered off chasing a rabbit and wouldn't come back. Stupidly I followed, trying to catch him, and managed to fall down a rabbit hole. Even more stupidly I left my phone at home.'

Gently Leo ran his hands over Mattie's leg and ankle. 'Hmm. Think you've only twisted it. Right. Plan of action.' He glanced up at Katie. 'You stay here with Mattie. I'll run back down and get the car. Think between us we'll manage to get her back up to the lane? Or do we need some extra help?'

'We'll manage,' Mattie said. 'Don't need official reinforcements.'

'I'll be as quick as I can,' Leo promised, placing his jacket around Mattie's shoulders, and then he was gone.

'I'll phone Henri and tell him we've found you,' Katie said. 'He's beside himself with worry.'

When Henri answered she quickly told him that Mattie was safe and should be home soon. Smiling she handed the phone to Mattie who reassured Henri personally that she was fine. 'Well, apart from a dodgy ankle,' she said. 'I'm so sorry you've been worried.'

Handing the phone back to Katie she said, 'Can you help me to my feet? We might as well try to get a bit closer to the lane before Leo gets back.'

Doubtfully Katie put her arm around Mattie and steadied herself as Mattie pushed hard against her and levered herself up, wincing as she did so.

'You OK?' Katie said gently. 'I still think it would be better to wait for Leo to come back and help.'

Mattie shook her head determinedly. 'I can hop slowly. The closer we can get to the lane the better.'

After a few hops that moved her all of five yards, Katie could sense that Mattie was tiring and regretting her insistence that she could manage but was refusing to say so.

'Listen. I can hear a car,' she said, making Mattie stand still. 'Leo will be here any moment.'

The headlights showed on the single-track lane but to Katie's disappointment continued past where she and Mattie were. It took her several seconds to realize that Leo would have continued to the car park at Coastguard Cottages to turn around. Lights coming back down the lane confirmed it.

A car door slammed and seconds later Leo appeared. 'Oh Mattie, I might have known I couldn't trust you to stay put,' and before she could protest, he'd swept her up in his arms and was carrying her over the remaining ground to the car.

'Can tell you're a trained fireman,' Mattie laughed. 'Used to rescuing people.'

Katie clambered into the back of the car, pulling Bert in beside her while Leo gently settled Mattie into the passenger seat.

'Right, we'll soon have you home,' he said. 'Sure you don't want to swing by the hospital and get a doctor to check out that ankle?'

'No. I'll put a cold compress on it. If it's no better in the morning then I promise I'll get it looked at,' Mattie said. 'But it will be,' she added confidently.

'Well, I'm sure Henri will have something to say about it, if it's not,' Katie said.

An ashen-faced Henri was waiting for them back at the cottage. Mattie insisted she was quite capable of hobbling indoors and there was no need for Leo to carry her from the car. 'Although I wouldn't mind a helpful arm to lean on,' she said.

Once she was safely indoors and Henri was fussing over her, Leo said. 'Look, I can't leave the car blocking Above Town any longer and as Katie and I were just about to have supper up at the farm when you raised the alarm, Henri, can you manage without us?'

'*Oui, certainment*. I will look after Mattie now,' Henri said. 'Thank you for finding her so quickly.'

As Leo and Katie left, Henri began applying a cold compress to Mattie's ankle. She winced at the coldness and the tightness with which Henri was applying it.

'I'm sorry, *ma chérie*, but it is better this way. You must stay sitting with your leg up on the stool. Now I pour you a brandy.'

'Henri, could I please have a cup of tea rather than brandy? I'm not particularly fond of it. Tea is so much more comforting.'

'You English and your love of tea,' Henri said, smiling. 'You think it is the cure for everything. OK, I make you tea but I shall have a brandy.'

Five minutes later as they sat drinking their respective drinks Henri sighed before saying, 'Honestly, Mattie, what am I going to do with you? Fancy chasing after Bert – you know he always comes back.'

Mattie sighed and tried to shift her position slightly. 'I know. I just wasn't thinking. No, that's not true. I was thinking but not about Bert.' She put her cup down on the saucer. 'I was thinking about that "real world" you were talking about earlier.'

Henri waited.

'I think I'd rather like to be a part of that world with you, Henri, if you'll have me,' Mattie said quietly, looking at him.

'I too have been thinking more about that,' Henri said. 'I think I was wrong.'

Mattie's heart plummeted. Had Henri changed his mind about her?

'I don't need to buy a house down south. There are lots of very good hotels down there for when we visit.'

'For a moment there I thought you'd changed your mind,' Mattie said, sighing with relief.

'Non, *ma chérie*. You're the best thing that has happened to me for many years. Tonight's *petit* adventure has made me more determined to take care of you. I think we will manage very well living between here and Paris,' Henri said. 'From now on we do things together.'

TWENTY-SIX

'How's Mattie today?' Leo asked as he and Katie drove to Blackawton the next evening.

'Bit sore and feeling silly for chasing after Bert, I think. Henri is being marvellous with her – so patient. He's cancelled their tickets to Paris until Mattie's ankle is better.'

Leo was driving fast, on the edge of the speed limit. 'Hey, we're in a bit of a hurry aren't we?' Katie said as the tall hedges on either side of the country lane flew past. 'Can we slow down, please? You're not on a shout-out now.'

'Don't like my driving?' Leo said.

'Just don't want you to get a speeding ticket,' Katie said. Not that there were likely to be any cameras around here. Going fast on the motorway was one thing but down these narrow country lanes was another.

'Sorry,' Leo said. 'I just want to get there and find out what this is all about.'

'I've never been to Ron's farm,' Katie said.

'It's a bit of an eyesore,' Leo said. 'He keeps a lot of old machinery around the place. And a fierce dog.'

The dog, asleep on the end of his chain when they drove

into the yard, woke and began barking frenziedly as Leo turned the car before parking it in front of the farmhouse.

'In case we need to make a quick getaway,' he said. 'Now where's Ron?'

Just then, Gary opened the front door. 'Oh, it's you two. Granddad said you might be around.'

'Is he here?' Leo asked.

'Yeah. Go on in. I'm off out to feed the sheep. Granddad's in the kitchen.'

Inside, the farmhouse was surprising clean and tidy. They found Ron sitting by the old-fashioned range in the kitchen, reading the betting page of a sports paper.

'You took yer time coming,' he said by way of greeting.

'So what's this all about, Ron?' Leo said.

'I need to tell you summat. You'm involved so I reckon you've the right to know.'

'It's about A Good Yarn, is it?' Katie said.

Ron nodded. 'I know them what's responsible for everything that's been happening down there.'

'Then you should be talking to the police not us,' Leo said.

'Can't,' Ron answered. 'They'd know who shopped 'em.'

'They?'

'Them as what is behind it all,' Ron said impatiently.

'So, who would that be?' Leo said.

'Developers.'

'Lake and Bidder?'

Ron nodded. 'Wanted to get their hands on the shop so they had the complete block. Figured it would be worth that much more.'

'Have you known this from the beginning?' Katie said.

Ron nodded. 'Hoped it would make you give up and Mattie finally cave in and sell. I'd get me money then. Thought I might as well keep quiet and benefit from their shenanigans as much as them. Trouble was, they knew it.'

'How?' Leo said.

'Pub talk,' Ron said briefly. 'Got a bit drunk one night and they latched on to the fact that I was what they called "an interested party". Talked me into going along with their plans. Said they'd see me all right if I kept shtum.'

'Did you do the actual vandalism, then?' Katie asked.

'No. I just watched and waited.'

'So why are you telling us now?' Katie said.

'I reckons they gone too far with that fire. Downright dangerous, that were. I ain't being involved with the likes of that. Someone could have been killed.'

'They caused the fire deliberately?' Katie said, her voice shaking.

Ron nodded. 'Says they've got a bit of a cash-flow problem. Figured they'd get the insurance money and frighten you out of A Good Yarn at the same time.'

'So now you've told us – what do you want us to do?' Leo said.

'Ain't nothing you can do,' Ron said. 'I just wanted you to know.'

'What about telling the police?' Leo said. 'We could come with you.'

'That won't do no good. Be their word against mine and we all know who the coppers would believe.'

'Actually, Ron, the forensic boys from the Fire Department are already investigating the fire,' Leo said.

'They'll know soon how the fire started and if it is foul play, they'll be straight on to the developers. The police will be involved then whether you like it or not.'

'Well, they won't get no information out of me,' Ron said. 'I didn't do it and as far as the police are concerned, I don't know nothing.'

'Have it your way,' Leo said. 'Anything else you want to tell us?'

Ron shook his head. 'Nope.'

'So, we can take it you won't personally be instigating any acts of vandalism in the future?' Leo said.

'Reckon Mattie still owes me,' Ron muttered. 'No. Gary tells me he wants to be a farmer so I'm going to let the lad have a crack at this place. He's promised to look after me in me old age – seeing as how I ain't got any money or me rights from the family.' He glared at them. 'Ain't got anything else to tell you so you can scarper now.' Ron picked up his racing paper and turned his back on them. 'You can see yerselves out.'

Katie was quiet as they took the road back to town. It was Leo who broke the silence.

'Well, at least we know there won't be any more trouble at A Good Yarn – which is something – but whether Ron will get away with not telling the police what he knows is another thing. Withholding information is not a good thing to be charged with.'

'You definitely think forensic will unearth the cause of the fire?'

Leo nodded. 'Very little gets past them these days.'

TWENTY-SEVEN

'Henri, I am not cancelling the Empreys this afternoon. I'm fine, honestly,' Mattie said. 'The cold compresses have worked wonders. The swelling has gone down a lot. I've been truly spoilt having you to look after me, thank you.'

Henri gave her a resigned smile, knowing she was determined. 'I still think you need to rest it more.'

'I promise I'll just sit here and let you do the host bit,' Mattie said. 'I'm so looking forward to seeing how their family tree ties in with mine. Which reminds me – I need to get the family box down from my room,' and she went to move from her chair.

'Mattie! *Non*! Don't even think about it. I'll get it. Tell me where it is and I fetch it for you.'

By the time Noah Snr arrived with Elizabeth and Vicky, the family box was on the sitting room table along with some other papers and books that Mattie thought might be of interest to Noah.

'No Noah Jnr today, then?' Mattie asked.

'He's got a hot date, ma'am, down with Trisha at the shop,' Noah snr. laughed. 'Katie is leaving them in charge for an hour while she joins us up here. I'll just put this down,' and he placed the shoe-sized box he'd been holding on the table, alongside Mattie's box.

Vicky handed Mattie some papers. 'This is our family tree so far. Look, this is the first mention of a Luttrell back in 1829.'

Mattie smiled. 'Amos the rogue vicar! Oh, there's a Cranford too.' She looked up at Noah and Elizabeth. 'We may have more relatives in common than you thought,' she said, taking a document out of her own family box and handing it to Vicky. 'This shows the family tree for my particular branch of the Cranfords.'

Katie arrived while they were all pouring over the two documents trying to work out the connections between the two families.

'I've brought some scones and cream,' she said. 'No, I know they won't be up to your standard, Mattie, but I figured you wouldn't have been allowed in the kitchen. I'll make some tea for everyone.'

By the time Katie returned with the tea and the scones, a definite link had been worked out between the Empreys and Mattie's branch of the Luttrells and Cranfords. Anne Follett, the woman Vicky had mentioned previously, proved to be the missing link.

'How exciting to have American relatives,' Katie said, looking at all the papers spread over the table. 'Even if they are ten or twelve times removed! What's in the unopened box, then?' she asked, looking at the one Noah had brought.

'Ah,' Noah said. 'That is something else entirely. It's something my mother needs to talk to Mattie about.'

Elizabeth glanced across at Mattie. 'My mother, Kitty, was a very private person. She never talked about her childhood or the loss of her twin brother, Nathaniel, in World War Two. She was of the belief you just got on with whatever life threw at you.' Elizabeth smiled at Mattie. 'I think you're like that too, aren't you?'

'Mattie is a firm believer in the past being the past,' Katie said.

'No point in being otherwise about things you can't change,' Mattie said. 'Waste of energy. Do you remember your Uncle Nathaniel?'

Elizabeth shook her head. 'Vaguely. I was five when he enlisted and he never came back.'

She looked across at the box. 'Being twins my mother and her brother were extremely close and he wrote long letters home from Europe. She kept every one of them. They're in that box. Together with some photos.'

Noah took the lid off the box and began to lift out the contents. A photo fluttered out onto the table. Noah quickly picked it up and put it face down.

'Most of the letters are dated but because of security no location is given,' Noah said. 'They're mainly about how different he was finding life as a GI. These, though, will be more interesting to you,' and he lifted out a bundle of letters tied together with ribbon.

'These are the letters he wrote to "My darling sister Kitty", telling her about this wonderful English girl he'd met and who he was going to marry – after this damned war is over,' Noah continued.

'Mattie,' Elizabeth said, gently taking her by the hand. 'Before we go any further, you need to know that Nathaniel was always known as Hal in the family.'

There was a sharp intake of breath as Mattie stared at her wide-eyed. 'Are you telling me what I think you are?'

Elizabeth nodded. 'The Hal your sister Clara was in love with was my Uncle Nathaniel.'

Mattie shook her head. 'I can't believe it.'

'Look, Mattie,' Noah said, picking up the photo from the table and turning it over. 'This is them together. Very similar to the one you showed me. And, before you ask, I'd never seen a photo of my great-uncle before Vicky unearthed these. Great-grandma Kitty had put them all away before I was born. I had no idea when you showed me your photographs who I was looking at.'

Mattie could feel the tears starting to well up as she looked at the photo of Clara and Hal. 'They were so happy together. Your uncle was lovely.'

'You remember him well?' Elizabeth asked.

'Oh yes, he was very kind to me. I missed him so much when he died.' Mattie was silent for a moment, remembering. Nobody had thought to comfort her when the news came through about the tragedy.

'Although he was Clara's boyfriend, he was my friend too. Always gave me candy whenever I saw him – and piggybacks! Said I reminded him of home and his young niece.' Mattie stopped. 'He must have meant you,' she said, pointing at Elizabeth.

'Did you know Clara also wrote to my mother?' Elizabeth said.

Mattie shook her head. 'No.'

'Because Hal's letters were censored, he gave Clara our home address so she could write about all the things he wasn't allowed to. Those letters are in the box too. Apart from the first couple which were written before Operation Tiger and Hal's death, they were all written from somewhere in Somerset.'

'Have you read the letters?' Mattie asked.

'Yes – and I'll leave them with you to read,' Elizabeth said. 'I think my mother got great comfort from the contact she had with Clara, both before and after Hal's death,' Elizabeth added quietly.

'I can't believe this,' Mattie said. 'After all these years – to learn something like this.' She wiped some tears away with the back of her hand before Henri silently handed her his handkerchief.

'Did you know, according to the last few letters, Clara was planning to emigrate to America?' Elizabeth said. 'My mother wrote and invited her. Said she'd already started to think of her as a sister-in-law and she'd be more than welcome to be a part of our family, as if she and Hal had married. Apparently your parents weren't ...' she hesitated, 'as happy about the relationship as Clara was.'

'That's an understatement,' Mattie said. 'They were adamant that she was far too young to know what she was doing. They dismissed the idea of her loving Hal as rubbish. When he was killed, they assumed Clara would just accept it was over and get on with her life here without him.' Mattie sighed. 'Nothing was ever going to be the same again.'

'Her last letter to me is in my family box there,' she said. 'It was full of her plans for her new life somewhere – she didn't say where she was going, in case our parents read the letter, I suppose – but she did say I was to visit when she was settled.' Mattie bit her lip. 'It was while she was posting that letter to me she was killed.'

Elizabeth squeezed her hand. 'That must have been so hard for you to accept.'

Mattie nodded. 'But there was nobody to tell your mother about Clara's accident, was there?' she said. 'We didn't even know she existed. She must have wondered what had happened. Why the letters suddenly stopped, why the woman she thought of as her sister-in-law didn't arrive in America as they'd planned.'

'There's an unopened envelope here, in Great-grandma Kitty's writing,' Noah said quietly. 'The address has been crossed through and "Gone Away. Return to Sender" is written all over it.' Noah looked at Mattie.

'As it has this address on it, I think Great-grandma Kitty must have tried to reach Clara through this address when she failed to hear from her. Your parents must have sent it back, unopened and without an explanation.'

It was Elizabeth's turn to sigh. 'I imagine that was when Mother put everything, the letters, photos of Hal, in the box and put it away in the attic. She had to learn to live without Hal or the English woman he'd loved and whom she was destined never to meet. It was probably easier to lock things away and try to forget what might have been if the woman he'd loved had joined us.'

Mattie wiped her eyes with Henri's handkerchief. 'I'm so sorry, Elizabeth. I can only apologize for my parents' lack of compassion towards your family.'

TWENTY-EIGHT

Katie was busy in A Good Yarn over the next few days. With Mattie still taking it easy at Henri's insistence, Katie was glad Trisha was able to step in and work extra hours. Worldwide Knit in Public Day seemed to have generated a lot of interest both from locals and holidaymakers.

She was surprised on Saturday afternoon when the local florist arrived with a wreath of ivy and white and red poppies.

'Mattie ordered it for this evening's D-Day river trip,' the florist said.

Carefully, Katie placed the wreath in the clubroom. Should she have ordered one too? Maybe it was the done thing.

When Leo arrived later that day, ready to walk down to the boats with her, she mentioned it to him. 'Should I have ordered one? Does everyone throw one overboard?'

'Not usually. The vicar and perhaps the chairperson of one of the local societies. The harbour master isn't keen on too many floating objects!'

'Will there be many boats taking part in the ceremony?' Katie asked.

Leo shook his head. 'It gets less every year – unless it's a big anniversary like the 60th or 70th. Are Mattie and Henri coming here or are we meeting them on the quay?'

'They should be here soon – if they haven't come to blows.' Leo looked at her.

'Mattie is determined to walk down and Henri is equally determined she shouldn't and wants to book a taxi,' Katie said, laughing.

'Taxi? No chance. My money is on Mattie walking,' Leo said.

'Shall we wait outside for them? Oh, I mustn't forget the wreath,' and turning to fetch the garland, Katie handed the shop keys to Leo to lock up for her.

'Don't forget your fleece,' Leo called after her. 'It will be cooler on the river.'

Standing outside A Good Yarn, waiting for Mattie and Henri, Katie glanced at the fire-blackened buildings next door.

'We were so lucky not to have more damage,' she said. She glanced at Leo. 'Any news on the cause?'

'Definitely started deliberately, as Ron said,' Leo said. 'A full investigation is underway.'

'Wonder if that means Ron will be helping the police with their enquiries,' Katie said. 'He seemed determined to keep what he knew to himself.'

'Think he'll find he doesn't have any option but to tell the police what he knows. They can be very persuasive,' Leo said. 'Ah, I see Mattie got her own way – even if she did have to give in to using a walking stick!'

'Oh good, you've got the wreath,' Mattie said. 'Do you

mind carrying it for me? With this stick Henri insists I use I don't have a free hand. I feel like an old woman,' she grumbled. 'My ankle is so much better.'

'*Bon*,' Henri said. 'And that's the way we want to keep it. I'll carry the wreath, Katie,' and he took it from her carefully. 'Your godmother is a very stubborn woman,' he added with a smile.

'Where are we boarding Michael's boat?' Mattie asked. 'Usual pontoon by the Station Cafe?'

'Yes,' Leo answered. 'We'd better get a move on – he'll be wanting to get going in about twenty minutes.'

When they arrived at the pontoon, Noah Snr was on board Michael's boat, the *Nicola-Suzanne*, with his large video camera on his shoulder, filming people as they arrived.

'I hope you don't mind,' he said. 'It's for the final part of my documentary. I want to include the way D-Day is commemorated in the twenty-first century.'

Elizabeth and Vicky were already on board and made room for Mattie by them on the seat in the bow. Katie and Henri stayed standing nearby while Leo went to give his father a hand casting off the mooring ropes, before joining him in the cockpit while he negotiated the boat away from the pontoon to follow the small flotilla of boats making their way downriver.

As the boats moved towards the twin castles at either side of the mouth of the river, Mattie started to point things out to Henri and Elizabeth.

'Look, you can see my cottage from here,' she said, pointing towards the shoreline. 'The top window you can see is the bedroom you're in, Henri. It's the room I spent all day in watching the harbour empty in 1944.' She paused. 'So many boats. Even now I can remember thinking it would have been possible to cross to Kingswear jumping from boat to boat.'

'You didn't go down to the quay to watch and wave them goodbye?' Elizabeth asked. 'I would have expected there to be crowds of people all along the embankment.'

Mattie shook her head. 'Not allowed to. It was all still very hush-hush. Also, there were hundreds of tanks and troops pouring into town. Everyone was ordered to stay indoors out of harm's way. It took all day to clear the harbour. I remember thinking the day was never going to end. And that was before I learnt that Clara had disappeared,' she added quietly.

'The logistics of organizing the 485 boats and all the troops that left here that fateful morning must have been huge,' Henri said thoughtfully.

'It's hard to accept that fewer people were killed on the actual beach landings the next day in Normandy than in Operation Tiger here in the South Hams,' Noah Snr said sadly. 'Seems all wrong somehow.'

Everybody fell silent at his words, remembering how Operation Tiger had altered the dynamics of their own lives even before D-Day had happened.

It was cold out on the river and as the boats neared the open waters of the channel Katie was glad of her fleece. When Leo joined her and placed his arm around her shoulders, holding her tight, she leant against him, glad of the additional warmth from his body.

Once the flotilla of boats were safely past the Mewstone, with its attendant cormorants, boat engines were briefly silenced. On board the *Nicola-Suzanne* they watched as the vicar threw the official wreath into the sea from the harbour master's boat. His words of dedication, though, were carried away on the wind that was springing up.

Mattie took her wreath from Henri and looked at Elizabeth. 'Would you like to help me throw this?' she asked softly. 'For Hal and Clara.'

Elizabeth, her eyes brimming with tears, nodded. 'Yes.'

Together they held and raised the wreath before dropping it over the starboard side of the *Nicola-Suzanne* and watching as it was caught up in the waves of the turning tide and began to float out into the channel proper.

With Elizabeth on one side and Henri on the other, all watching the wreath with its red and white poppies being buffeted on the water, Mattie said quietly, 'Out of past sorrows we will forge new friendships.'

Henri gave her hand a conciliatory squeeze and Elizabeth whispered, 'We will.'

A minute later, boat engines were switched back into life and the flotilla started its return journey. The throwing of the wreath seemed to have lightened the atmosphere on board. Somehow it was as if the sadness that had accompanied them out to sea had been thrown away with the wreath and been replaced with the expectation that things would be better from now on.

An early-evening sea mist began to swirl in as they motored back in, swathing the castle and St Petrox Church in wispy white fronds.

'You know Castle Farm is in St Petrox's parish, don't you?' Leo murmured to Katie as she looked at the ancient monument. 'I can get married there if I want to.'

Katie turned to look at him. 'And do you want to?'

'Definitely,' Leo said. 'Come into the stern. I want to make sure you see something,' he said, taking her by the hand.

Obediently, Katie went with him, glad of his steadying hand as the boat ploughed through the water.

'You get the best view from here,' Leo said, standing behind her and wrapping his arms around her. 'Look over there, towards the left shore.'

It took Katie several seconds to see what he was getting at. 'Oh, that's so beautiful,' she said as she finally saw the graceful bronze mermaid serenely sitting on the rocks. 'What a perfect place for her.'

'She's been there a few years now,' Leo said quietly. 'Every time I'm out on the river and see her, I think of you. Perfect – but elusive.' He turned her in his arms and looked at her seriously for several seconds. 'Are you ready to stop being elusive and marry me in St Petrox, Tiggy?'

Katie smiled. 'Yes. That would be the perfect part.'

'Success is not final, failure is not fatal,
It is the courage to continue that counts.'

WINSTON CHURCHILL